A MOUTHFUL
OF TONGUES

HER TOTIPOTENT TROPICANALIA

A MOUTHFUL
OF TONGUES

Published by:

Cosmos Books, an imprint of Wildside Press
www.cosmos-books.com
www.wildsidepress.com

Copyright © 2002 by Paul Di Filippo
Cover art "The Kiss of the Sphinx" by Franz von Stuck
Cover design copyright © 2002 by Garry Nurrish

For more information, contact Wildside Press.

ISBN: 1-58715-506-9

A MOUTHFUL OF TONGUES

HER TOTIPOTENT TROPICANALIA

PAUL DI FILIPPO

COSMOS BOOKS

FOR DEBORAH
She saw, she came, she conquered.

"How I have wept—for a whole night, sometimes—over the poor women of olden days, women who were so beautiful, so tender, so gentle, women who opened wide their arms ready to receive a kiss—and now they are dead! The kiss itself is immortal. It travels from mouth to mouth, from century to century, from age to age. Men and women receive kisses, give kisses—and die."
    —Guy de Maupassant, "The Head of Hair".

"[T]he erogenous zones ... might equally well be termed *gnoseogenous*, for they communicate not only pleasure, but also the *knowledge* of reality."
    —Erich Neumann, *The Child*.

"He was apprehensive because he had introduced thinly-drawn characters who moved about in a demented world and could never be convincing."
    —Georges Bataille, *L'Abbé C.*

PART ONE

Into that dream again. That deep, dark, dangerous dream.

Matted mulch underfoot, crisping with each barefoot step she tentatively takes, stubs of twigs and empty seed pods prickling her soles. Tinted sunlight welding leaf to stem in the thick slotted living canopy above, brazing corrugated tree trunks, ricocheting off dangling fruits and nuts, tangling in hairy thickets, dripping in amber sparkles off the arcs of lianas. Secret language of insects droning hieratically in her ears, bird calls like cryptic commentary punctuating her passage. Moist air cottoning against her—unclothed? yes, completely unclothed—body.

Step by step the fecund jungle lures her deeper within itself. For an indeterminate time, confidence and pleasure swell within her. Her hands stretch joyously out to either side to caress warm golden boles and waxy jade foliage. She kneels to lap aromatic rainwater from the impossibly clean ciborium of a pitcher plant, pistils tickling her nose. Lugubrious lizards lunge from hot plates of stone to shelter beneath welcoming tented fronds. A parrot with a red-streaked beak jitters along from branch to branch parallel with her chance-dictated course, winking at her with cocked head. Butterflies large as women's dainty handkerchiefs and stitched as prettily shimmer round her momentarily before dispersing.

Then she chances upon the lone fat bold paw-print, blazoned into a square of bare soil.

The sun pulls a passing cloud before its frightened face. An unseen beast coughs roughly. A banded snake

13

slips across the trail, a squiggle of movement linking two absences. A monkey laughs. The paw-print seems to swell in her sight until it fills her whole field of vision, freezing the day, its negative space conjuring up the instrument that stamped it: four strong clawed toes, rough palm-pad wide as a cup's saucer, dew-claw that dragged a thin line in the dirt.

Three or six grains of sand crumble from the edge of the print into its receptive depression, restoring time. Suddenly frantic, she begins to run.

Now the jungle does not invite, but hinders. Branches slap her arms, raising welts. Thorns needle her flanks. The concealed mouths of rodent burrows invite broken ankles. Trees slide closer together to bar her passage.

Her breath rasps from her lungs. Sweat stings her eyes. Her tongue captures a trickle of blood meandering lazily over her upper lip like the first drops rilling from an ineffective dike.

She crashes out of a wall of whipping foliage into a broad short-grassed clearing. Exposed, she realizes too late her fatal mistake. She tries to go back, but the withy latticed curtain now defies penetration. Hopeless, she starts to sprint across the clearing toward some theoretical safety.

Halfway across, she risks a compulsive look backwards.

The jaguar has emerged.

Bigger than her, its massive presence dominating the clearing like a fallen chunk of starless space, the kingly cat wears its black fur like a garment woven of pure night. Despite the gap between the woman and the animal, the cat's features fill her sight to the exclusion of all else: its whiskers, thick and lucid as fiberoptics, stretch a foot to either side of its blunt muzzle; its garnet eyes glitter; its nostrils flare wetly; its throat pulses with the rude vigor of its heartbeat. A tongue like a velvet washcloth strops up, around, and down before disappearing. A tail like the sinuous scribble sketched offhandedly onto canvas by an old master lashes the stolid air.

Nearly paralyzed with anticipatory fear, the cat's image bonded to her soul, she tries to resume her run, stumbles after only a few yards, and falls to hands and knees.

A MOUTHFUL OF TONGUES

Instantly the jaguar is upon her, atop her, cloaking her like a heavy cape, its weight immense. She is too terrified even to scream.

She tenses for the bite that will sever her spine at the neck.

The slash of teeth never comes. Slowly, acid sweat burning her armpits and some small sanity returning, she catalogs finer impressions.

The jaguar's forelimbs compress her ribs below her flooded armpits, furry staves barrelling her torso. The cat's heavy head lolls on her right shoulder, its left ear cupped to her right one like mated shells; should she turn, she suspects her eyes would lock with its slitted pupils. Warm meaty breath washes her cheek. The jaguar's muscled back legs clamp hers from the outside, and a dew-claw digs into one calf, causing the only pain.

Then she feels a ponderous, prescient unsheathing between the cheeks of her ass.

The jaguar's stiffening prick emerges from its furry case, already juiced and thick. A knot as big as twin walnuts swells in the penis, much closer to the root than the tip. The hot length of the cat's member seems to lay a brand on her sensitive flesh. She feels her traitorous cunt responding with lubrications that make no distinctions between man and beast.

Still gripping her, the jaguar backs up delicately an inch at a step, until its bristly chin rests on her nape. The pointed tip of its prick slides inerringly down her crack, slurring fluid, snagging a millisecond on the ridged rim of her asshole, finally coming to rest between her cunt's fiery lips.

The jaguar bucks, and its cock slides in up to the knot. She screams, falls forward from the waist. Then the cat pushes all the way in.

The right cheek of her face now cushioned on the grass, her nipples scribing the turf, she and the jaguar fuck.

Each time the knot is pulled out or pushed in, a wordless plosive exclamation escapes her. Her inner cunt lips invert on the inward stroke and evert on the outward.

The jaguar's thrusts accelerate, and resonant undulations quake her buttocks. One final almost unbearable ramming triggers both the cat's cum and her own titanic climax.

When the scalding fluid generously geysers up her—every drop contained within her uterine channels due to the knot's blockage—the slumber-hosted transformation instantly begins. She feels her limbs melt and reconfigure, her torso elongate, her face reshape.

Within seconds, the lovers have collapsed to the verdant grass, two lithe black jaguars, one large, one small, lying entwined, licking each other's muzzles beneath the sun.

Kerry Hackett awakes. Her dream orgasm quivers out its final fading traces along her bare limbs, ripples in her midriff. A flush spreads like a radiant gorget around her neck and upper bosom. So hot she has to kick the covers off, despite the apartment's wintry unheated chill. (Electricity rationing again till noon today.) Her autonomous cunt's made a soppy wet spot on the sheets. Will Tango notice? Doubtful, since the big man continues to sleep so soundly on his own side of the bed, like a semi-gaunt yet still wanly handsome corpse awaiting the tender ministrations of an embalmer.

The bedside clock reads a crimson six-thirty, half an hour away from its appointed shrilling. Kerry shuts off the alarm and slides out of the bed. The wood floor insults her bare feet, so she hastens to the bathroom, where at least a cotton mat interfaces between self and world.

In the lighted chamber, behind shut door, her breath plumes. On the chill toilet, she laves ceramic bowl with steaming piss. No toilet paper again, under dual constraints of meager money and short supply. No matter, since she'll soon have a hot shower—assuming the city's natural gas supply hasn't been interrupted once more.

Before arising from the toilet, she checks for signs of her imminent period. Not yet.

Kerry cajoles hot water out of the sink tap, untenses muscles braced to receive only cold, and scrubs her face with suds from a sliver of yellowing soap. Dropping the towel from her face, she confronts herself in the mirror: short peltish black hair feathered across a high brow, cornflower-blue eyes, smallish nose, full wide lips, a pugnacious chin. But a portion of her features are swamped in noise: an enormous port-wine birthmark, permanent love-bruise from the gods, damage from a clumsy stork, sprawls across half her visage, a map of some terra incognita occluding an asymmetrical portion of forehead, nose, left eye-socket, cheek and jaw.

In the shower, Kerry soaps thoroughly, scrubbing hard between her legs as if to wash her recurrent dream away. She mashes her cunt as if to squeeze out the semen of the dream jaguar—or perhaps to drive it deeper in. Despite erotic satiation, her own touch is mildly arousing, and her nipples react. She offs the shower and steps out. The fall of water from her high-jutting breasts resembles the drip of light from the lianas in the oneiric jungle.

She brushes her teeth with raw baking soda and hydrogen peroxide, granular paste cupped in her palm. In the steamy mirror, she applies minimal makeup: frosted eyes, iced lips to match her painted nails.

Back in the bedroom, guided only by spill of bathroom light, Kerry dresses quickly. Azure bra and matching panties, black stockings that elastically grip her thighs up high where they narrow and tauten. Her second-best suit, the brown one, seems cleanest. A gold chain once her mother's fits tightly around her sculpted neck, accessorizing her outfit bravely but without companionship of other jewelry. Old cloth coat with faux fur collar, boots suitable for snowy streets, sensible flats in her carry-bag. She picks up her wallet from the dresser and plumbs its disappointing depths, finally plucking out one of her last two NUfives. She pins the nudie bill under Tango's six prescription vials on the galley table, where he's certain to encounter it.

Her lover still sleeps, face pillow-buried. Kerry sighs, plants a perfunctory kiss on the back of his head, then leaves the apartment without breakfast or goodbyes.

Poorly brightened by a yellow bulb, the ground-floor vestibule—full of wind-sifted litter, its smashed-lock outer door ajar an inch—holds a dozing beggar cocooned in a greasy blue U-Haul blanket, nothing much showing except his tubercular bearded face, so grimy as to render his race and age indeterminate. The polyester chrysalis shifts as Kerry attempts to sidestep it, one of the beggar's rheumy eyes open, and a frost-blackened hand extends.

"Spare change, miss?"

Kerry unpockets a mixed handful of new tin and old silver and dribbles the small offering into the cupped calloused palm.

"The gods bless you, lady."

Kerry cracks the door wider, until it nearly scrunches the beggar's blanketed feet, and steps outside.

Dawn's fighting vicious battalions of gunmetal clouds. Week-old snow, rendered into a semblance of soot-swirled eroded plastic, heaps against basement windows, clings in compressed sidewalk patches seemingly designed as ankle-wrenching pedestrian hazards. Kerry descends ten broken steps carefully, pulls her coat more closely around her, then begins her walk to work.

Half-reassuringly, half-worrisomely, National Guard patrols are omnipresent this morning, camouflaged stalkers in the urban jungle. In pairs and threesomes, featuring the occasional quartet, they warily make their random rounds through the neighborhood, sleek rifles carried lightly like sheaves of grains in the arms of rustic celebrants. (The four-person squads among them also lug the shared components of a crazy-foam riot-buster.) The young Guards, male and female alike, eye Kerry neutrally, and she correspondingly maintains a head-held-high, gaze-straight attitude.

Vehicular traffic is almost nonexistent, save for a lurching methanol-powered bus, a limo, and a few powered trikes.

At an intersection, Kerry flinches as the possible yet improbable sound of sniper fire reaches her, a rattle of low-caliber snaps. But the easy-striding fellow pedestrians further along her intended path do not seem to be scurrying for cover, so she cautiously proceeds. The mock-assault discloses itself: a construction crew is boarding up with plywood sheets a still-steaming building on Shepard Street, the pop of their nail-guns simulating attack.

A block from work, Kerry purchases her breakfast from a vendorless cart: a shrink-wrapped bagel, pre-sliced and -smeared, and a paper cup of herbal tea. After accepting three nudie singles from her, the cart scoots off, obeying programmatic rhythms of consumer enticement.

An innocuous office building marks her destination. A row of discreet bronze signs near the doors detail the tenants. Kerry's eyes flick to one: DIAVERDE PARABIOLOGICALS. In the small groundfloor atrium, Kerry nods to the building's receptionist and to several armed private guards, some roaming while two remain sealed away in a defensive booth. Resting hygienic bagel atop hot lidded cup, she thrust her free hand into a wall-mounted scanner's mouth. Stealing a few flakes of dead skin, the scanner performs an instant verification of her dual-helixed selfhood, and confirms by several additional tests that her hand is still attached to its rightful body. As a consequence, an elevator opens and beckons her in.

Diaverde occupies the tenth through fifteenth floors of the building; Kerry disembarks on the top level, administrative. The elevator discharges directly into a second reception area. Behind a small desk sits one of Kerry's co-workers, a pretty young black woman with glistening Josephine-Baker-revival hair and large-hooped earrings, dressed with low-budget elegance. The clock inset before the receptionist reads just eight. The black woman glances at the readout, then says, "You're early."

"Couldn't sleep. He in yet, Oreesha?"

"I don't think so. But who can be sure with the Phantom Boss?"

"Maybe I'll take a few minutes to eat then. I feel almost faint."

"Go for it, child. Say, you see that building got burned on Shepard?"

"Sure. What's the story?"

"Take your pick. Top two rumors are it was either a bomb-factory that had an accident, or a honey hive."

"If it'd been a honey hive, the Guard would've left nothing standing."

Oreesha shrugs, shoulders bumping hoops. "Maybe they're slacking off. Maybe they figure dirty honey's no good to anyone."

"Whatever. I've got too much on my mind to worry about it."

Kerry's small office intervenes between Oreesha's workstation and the quarters of their boss. She sets her breakfast down on her neatly ordered desktop, powers up her computer, shucks her coat, swaps boots for shoes from her carryall, and sits. Within seconds her monitor hosts Diaverde's Escherian corporate screen-saver: a leaf metamorphosing into a fish, fish into crab, crab into bird, bird into man, man into leaf, forever. Kerry glances over her shoulder at the golden door bearing her boss's name and title: PETER JARIUS, DIRECTOR. Nothing stirs within. She uncaps her tea, uncondoms her bagel, and breakfasts with tidy bites and sips.

Kerry's sorting through e-mail from the division heads, dealing with the less important memos, prioritizing and flagging the others for later reading by her boss, when she hears the door behind her open.

"Ms. Hackett, may I see you in my office, please?"

Kerry stiffens involuntarily, her hand coming up instinctively to splay across her facial maculation, slim white fingers striping purple epidermis. Heat scalds her palm. She forces herself to relax, to lower her hand. Without turning, she answers, "Yes, Mr. Jarius." She logs off—policy when leaving one's desk, even if only momentarily, even if under ostensibly secure conditions—picks up her PDA, and enters Jarius's office through the unlatched door.

Jarius has already resumed his seat behind an expensively modest desk, backed by a vast expanse of smoky glass offering a panorama of the raddled neighborhood. Today his tailored, collarless suit is a fashionable burgundy so dark as to appear nearly crow-black. Jarius's goatee, sideburns and quiff of thick hair are rusty roan streaked with grey. His complexion is swarthy and pocked with minute old acne scars. Teeth white as limestone in gums pink as grapefruit flesh stand forth when Jarius unleashes a smile on his secretary. His voice holds a rain-barrel resonance. Jarius's eyes traverse Kerry's whole form like inquisitive insect feelers before settling on her face—on her blemish?

"Ms. Hackett, you look particularly graceful today in that tasteful outfit."

Kerry's unmarked moiety of face colors a fraction of a step closer to matching the mottled portion. "It's certainly nothing I haven't worn before."

"Well, today it's a particularly effective business costume. You see, we have some unexpected visitors due here soon—several Senators on an inspection tour—and since you'll be helping me conduct the tour, as well as accompanying us all to dinner tonight, your looks are vital. Not, of course, that you ever appear less than professional and demure."

"Dinner? Tonight? But I had plans—"

Jarius negates her trivial plans with a negligent wave. "You'll simply have to cancel them. I can't be expected to manage these inquisitive federal boors all on my own. What if they ask me for statistics, costs, figures? Those are your metier, Ms. Hackett, part of your ultra-competent provenance." Jarius smiles again. "Face it, Ms. Hackett, as my personal secretary, you're indispensable to me."

"I'll have to call home."

Jarius frowns, a balked demiurge. "If you don't mind a slight personal inquisition, may I ask if you're still sharing a residence with that fellow you brought to the Christmas party last month? A Mr. Santangelo, I believe his name was . . . "

"Yes, I am. Why do you ask?"

Jarius mimes a faint distaste. "Just that you and he seem so dissonant together. He's rather—well, ragged and rough for a woman of your refinement."

"Things have gone hard for him lately. Tango's a good man."

"'Tango.' A rather childish nickname."

Kerry remains silent. Jarius says, "Is he still suffering like so many other unfortunates from his, ah, affliction?"

"Yes."

"And still taking his various medicines, those semipotent panaceas by which our rivals hold pitiful patients hostage? We wouldn't want you to succumb to your boyfriend's unrestrained bugs, should he desist from his protocol."

"I make sure he takes everything he's supposed to."

"Those pills are rather expensive, aren't they? Even with partial insurance coverage, they take a good chunk out of your pay, I estimate . . . "

"We get by."

"Well, perhaps I might engineer a slight raise for you, Ms. Hackett, considering how you always devote one hundred and ten percent to Diaverde. You're a fine employee. And I feel we understand each other magnificently well."

"Thank you, Mr. Jarius."

Jarius checks his watch, emergent from beneath link-clasped cuff. "Well, the Senators will be here in slightly over an hour. I expect you'll want to load your handy little pocket machine with all sorts of impressive data. Ms. Presser will alert us both when they arrive."

Jarius spins his chair to gaze out the window, effectively dismissing Kerry.

Back at her desk, Kerry sits silently for a minute, hands folded in her lap, before she uses her Diaverde-issued cellphone to call home. Her machine, not Tango, answers, spiels, and beeps. "Hello, Tango, it's me. Are you there? Pick up, please." No human intervention forestalls the machine's serene vacancy. She records a brief explanation for her unanticipated and unavoidable lateness home that night. She mates her PDA to her desk computer and uploads data on a range of current projects. By the time she finishes that chore and a few others, Oreesha is ushering in the Senators, and Jarius has emerged from his office. Hearty introductions all around, among the Diaverde people and the four Senators, three men and a woman. The latter share a generic bulkiness, due to lightweight yet effective armor hidden under their official grey legislative robes.

Jarius familiarly grips the senior Senator, the woman, by her elbow and steers her and her comrades toward the elevator. Kerry trails the pack.

"We have marvels aplenty to show you, Senator Ferryway," Jarius trumpets. "Exciting parabiological developments that will reward taxpayer investment a thousandfold."

Ferryway looks around suspiciously, as if checking for eavesdroppers. "We're particularly interested in Project Benthos."

Jarius positively glows. "Some astounding implications there. But not for general release to the public, of course."

"Of course."

Kerry scrolls up a directory of files on her PDA. There is no entry for any Project Benthos.

With Jarius frequently turning to Kerry for support, the next few hours are filled with demonstrations, interviews with staff scientists, computer simulations, performances by surly lab animals, soporific slide shows, lectures, and a lunch break in the company cafeteria. Over coffee, the Senators exhibit a suitable factoid-generated numbness, save for Ferryway, who bores in on her first concern.

"You've saved Project Benthos until last, I see."

A MOUTHFUL OF TONGUES

"Quite true, Senator. The last shall be first. Ha, ha, if I may be so religiously cryptic! Shall we go?"

One wing of the tenth floor is sealed off, entry determined by a hand-scanner. Before Jarius can trigger their entrance, Senator Ferryway casts a cold eye on Kerry. "Is your secretary cleared for this?"

In the fervency of his answer, Jarius seems almost more intent on impressing Kerry than on reassuring the Senator. "Why, of course she is. In fact, she has complete access to this wing. Ms. Hackett, if you would—"

Jarius is gesturing to the security device. Haltingly, Kerry mates her hand to the surface of a detector she has never before utilized.

Solenoids in the door retract with solid thunks.

Jarius bows the Senators in first. As they enter the Project Benthos area, he bestows behind their backs a sly smile on bewildered Kerry.

"I'll explain later, my dear," Jarius whispers to her.

Beyond the thick steel door, a sprinkling of technicians and scientists occupy themselves at intricate workstations resembling individualized factories, or perhaps the stacked reef habitats of reclusive sea-creatures. Kerry recognizes large-scale titration devices, Helios gene-guns, cyrogenic Dewars, ultrasonic autoclaves, DNA-sequencers and protein-linkers, but a host of more obscure machinery fails to correspond to any label she possesses. The skilled workers look up briefly, acknowledging the visitors, then return to their alchemical labors, save for one man, a burly dark-haired fellow with the mien of a shambling circus bear. He advances toward Jarius with a tentative smile.

"Dr. Teague, our friends would like to view the fruits of your ingenious labors."

Teague radiates authentic pleasure, plainly relishing this unwonted attention from important laypeople. "Ah, you've come to see the benthic. Very good, very good. Follow me."

On the far side of the lab, an interior window grants a view into a small sealed room. A pair of remote-manipulator gloves extrude into the airtight enclosure. A joystick and several simple buttons flank the glove cuffs on the humans' side of the partition. Stickers depicting the familiar wheel-like labrys of the biohazard trefoil are pasted at several points.

Teague positions himself at the controls, quickly jabs two buttons and wambles the joystick. Beyond the window, a robot trolley begins to move toward a rising hatch similar to a dumbwaiter door.

"The benthic," explains Teague, "is a literally unique creature, the only entity composed of one hundred percent realtime totipotent cells. It lives in a scrupulously controlled environment that replicates many human physiological parameters. We can decant it into its observation container for only a short time."

Something very like a small lidded aquarium studded with monitoring devices is sliding out of the hatch on a metal tongue and thence onto the trolley. Teague next maneuvers the trolley with its cargo before the window. The contents of the liquid-filled observation vessel become apparent.

Velvet golden-magenta convolutions, a welter of amorphous limbs, rugosely flocked, writhe with fluid grace, alternately shyly hiding and boldly revealing finer hairlike, hooklike or papillary structures. Coiling and uncoiling with languid strength, teasingly half-illuminating more recondite assemblages, casting fairy-delicate pseudopods and tendrils out only to reel them in, the strange asymmetrical uncentered creature conceals its true form in its extravagant display, a dancer clad with diaphanous yet impenetrable veils. The benthic seems to mass only as much as a housecat, but judging by its variable sinuosity, might very well be capable of spreading and flattening to cover the floor of a good-sized room.

Kerry can't remove her gaze from the fractally hypnotic creature. Its beauty nearly disables her lungs' autonomic functioning. Like a matador's empty supple suit of lights come alive, the benthic sparkles in her vision. How could she have been sharing a building with this uncanny living artifact without sensing its pulsing aliveness even through several concrete floors?

The Senators appear equally taken aback by the alien presence. Ferryway finds her tongue first.

"It—it can do everything you claim for it?"

Jarius answers. "You've seen the videos, Senator. Did you suspect we were faking them?"

"No. But it was all so incredible to me."

Jarius's teeth gleam. "Diaverde specializes in producing precisely that reaction, Madame Senator."

A MOUTHFUL OF TONGUES

Without ever having used the manipulator gloves to reach inside the aquarium and fondle the swirling captive—an action Kerry had been half anticipating, half dreading—Teague interrupts. "I have to return the benthic to its homeostatic tank now."

"I think we've all seen enough," ventures Jarius, and, meeting with no demurral, conducts the party out of the high-security area.

The rest of the day passes hazily for Kerry. She surfaces from her ruminative fugue several times to find herself working as assiduously as usual. During three such instances she tries to reach Tango, but meets with no success. At last, quitting time trundles round; Oreesha sticks her brilliantined head into Kerry's office.

"The company limo's pulling up now for you and Mr. Jarius." The receptionist winks. "Do me a favor and order the most expensive item on the menu. The likes of you and me don't step out with the bigshots all that often."

"What if the most expensive thing is something I don't like?"

"Shit, girl, you *learn* to like it!"

Peter Jarius's limo always rolls down into a securely armored basement garage: street pickups invite terrorism. Kerry, coated and booted, waits nervously near the chauffered vehicle, its anonymous stone-visaged driver attentive behind the wheel, but not obsequious. Nearly half an hour after most of the Diaverde staff has cleared the building, Jarius steps off the elevator. Spotting Kerry, he smiles with his usual precise degree of expressiveness and quickly crosses to her.

"Terribly sorry to keep you penned in this chilly cement cloister, Ms. Hackett. The demands of upper management make me long for my humble days in the lab. Well, you know my importunate schedule as well as I do, so surely you'll excuse me."

"Of course."

Jarius takes one of her hands and pats it. "How does The Greedy Parrot sound to you?"

"I've only heard of it—"

"It's everything that the foolishly wagging tongues of those with more money than brains can tattle of—and more. Shall we?"

Jarius opens the door for her, she climbs onboard, and he moves to slip in the same door, forcing her to slide over and slightly ruck up her skirt. Jarius eyes her exposed legs without leering, as if to convey a kind of dispassionate worldly appreciation. She makes no awkward move to adjust her skirt, but only looks away, out the window.

The darkening streets of the city are already emptying, arcades where games of cynical disillusionment attract few customers. Patrols range the dusk. Kerry spots one brace of bandoliered bravos bullying a beggar: as they spin him about for frisking, Kerry notes a folded blue blanket twine-bound to his back like a makeshift pack.

The front entry to The Greedy Parrot offers a walled portico manned by armed guards to shield discharging cars. After exiting, Jarius crooks an arm to escort Kerry inside. The tophatted doorman, jovial black Caribbean face matching his cocoa-rich voice, tugs open the heavy glass door, saying, "Mighty bitter out here, friends. Hurry inside."

Lemon-celery lighting, faux palm trees, animatronic wildlife, digitized jungle soundtrack, piped-in scents, and delicate random sprays of aromatic mist from the ceiling, enough to sheen faces lightly and dampen the expensive coiffures. The staff of servers is all-female, each sporting a duster of feathers from her rump and a cranial ruff, their bosomy low-cut, cheekily high-cut costumes hummingbird-bright.

Kerry and her boss are delivered to a small table with only two chairs.

"Where are the Senators going to sit?"

An innocent smile divides Jarius's past-poxed face. "Our illustrious legislators were summoned unexpectedly back to Ottawa. Their regretful call was what kept me so late in the office. But when I came down and saw you waiting so earnestly, I simply couldn't bear to cancel our much-anticipated outing."

Kerry does not take her seat. "I—I should leave now. This isn't right."

Jarius sighs dramatically. "Ms. Hackett, is it possible that you would deny me, one of your most familiar co-workers, the innocent pleasure of your afterhours company? Have you never previously enjoyed a drink with, say, Ms. Presser, at the end of a long hard day? Surely you'll grant me the same friendly privilege."

"I just don't know . . . "

A MOUTHFUL OF TONGUES

Stagily, Jarius presses a fingertip to the hinge of his jaw, as if pondering a possibility. "Is Mr. Santangelo perhaps waiting loyally for your return, with your homecooked supper steaming upon the table?"

Kerry frowns, and hesitates before answering. "I haven't been able to reach him all day."

Jarius claps his hands together triumphantly. "It's settled then. Please, rest your weary limbs upon this admirably cushioned chair, and let our solicitously hovering sommelier describe the wonders of his cellar. He appears ready to burst with pride."

Within minutes, Kerry is sipping a wine more redolent and flavorful than any she has ever before tasted, berry-tart, oak-sharp. Jarius is regaling her with witty anecdotes about the high and mighty, people known to her only from headlines. The invisible net of stress held visibly in her shoulders begins to unknot, the worry lines marring her birth-blotched pretty face dissolve into looser configurations. By her third glass she is laughing frequently at Jarius's mordant observations. The arrival of an appetizer of oysters brings a precarious halt to their conversation. Kerry casts a wary gaze on the shell-cradled lozenges of opalescent marine flesh, but upon hearty urging from Jarius, she samples the first one tentatively, then proceeds to enjoy her share heartily.

"Bravo, my dear! Always go forward bravely to encounter that which frightens you."

"I wish I could, Mr. Jarius."

"Please, Kerry—Peter."

"Peter, then."

As large, decoratively sauce-drizzled plates incommensurate with their scanty cargoes arrive, Jarius dabs at his lips with his crimson linen napkin, pinning Kerry with a keen scrutiny. Finally he inquires, "Tell me, my dear. What do you wish for during this short life we all share? What are your dreams?"

Kerry sits back from the table, plainly considering the question seriously. She crosses her legs, dandling one foot outside the tablecloth's curtain. "Gee, Peter, I don't know. A lot of the same things everyone wishes for. Enough money, a classier place to live, a better job—"

Jarius clutches his chest. "Aha! I'm a wicked troll, then, and Diaverde is a dank, dark, brutal mine!"

Kerry laughed. "No, not at all. But you have to admit my job is not the most creative one imaginable."

"Nor is mine. But without our hard work, chaos! However, those are all material things, more or less, even your imaginary perfect job. What are your spiritual dreams, your emotional desires? What secret ambitions dwell in the chambers of your heart? I'm truly interested."

"Well, I'd like to live in a less complicated, peaceful world—"

Jarius holds up one palm, his expression miming further hurt. "Don't tell me next that you want to help old people. Even though you're undeniably as glamorous as any Miss World candidate, I'm afraid I'll have to take offense."

"Oh, you're not old, Peter, so don't pretend you are just to get my sympathy."

"Caught dead to rights. I do desire your sympathy, Kerry. As well as other fond indulgences. That's why I granted you admittance to Project Benthos. As a token of my esteem. But please, continue."

"Oh, I don't know how to really explain what I sometimes feel. I long for a world that's—that's almost primitive. Someplace half-wild, green and tropical, where feelings and issues, needs and solutions are clear and uncomplicated. A place of real freedom, where I can feel things deeply and richly."

"Feel such things as love, perhaps?"

"Yes."

"And lust?"

Kerry picks up her fork and toys with the remnants of her food for a moment before answering more or less into her plate, "Of course."

A dessert trolley rolls up under the impulse of a parrot-woman. The half-familiar oscillations of a quivering molded pudding catch Kerry's eye, and she pulls back involuntarily but undeniably from the cart of offerings. Composing herself, she chooses an earth-dark slice of chocolate cake. Jarius, meanwhile, has ordered liqueur-spiked coffees for them both.

When they rise to leave, Kerry performs an impromptu awkward fandango with her chair before regaining control of her feet. Instantly, Jarius is by her side, steadying her with an arm around her waist.

A MOUTHFUL OF TONGUES

"Allow me, Kerry sweetling. Alcohol runs colder in these old veins than in your youthful arteries. My heart learned satiation long ago, while yours still imbibes too wildly."

"Oh, Mr. Jarius—sorry, Peter, sorry—you really can turn a phrase."

"Always better to turn a phrase than an ankle, my dear."

Kerry giggles, and they depart the artificial grotto of The Greedy Parrot.

Night, cold, the stacked cyclopean eyes of traffic lights, the blat of carhorns, and then the chauffeur is opening the limo's door at their destination, another underground garage. Kerry rides an elevator up several floors, each chiming sweetly in passing, leaning on the elegant slim form of Peter Jarius, whose arm continues to enfold her waist. The mummy-colored rug inside his twilit apartment seems ankle-deep.

"Feel free to discard those cumbersome galoshes, Kerry. This woolly sea longs to lap at your trim ankles."

Kerry crosses in stockinged feet to a buttery leather couch, spins giddily and drops melodramatically down. "What a wonderful evening! Such a pleasant change of pace."

Jarius tends bar in a clinking of glassware, his back to her. "I feel we both waited much too long to reward ourselves with such a simple tryst. But let us not dwell on our foolish past sins of omission."

Jarius's by her side on the couch, drinks in hand. Kerry accepts hers, sips, then sighs.

"Peter, you've been so considerate toward me."

"What you've experienced so far is but a token of my intense affections, dear."

Kerry draws a deep draught of her peaty drink, lowers glass to lap, rests her head backwards against warm cushions, then closes her eyes for a moment. Opening them, she finds Jarius unbuttoning her thin brown suitjacket.

"I want you to relax more fully, my dear. And of course I want a view of your splendid young breasts, so often admired from across the distance of authority that cruelly separates us."

Kerry neither cooperates nor resists. The scalloped blue lace of her bra against her pale skin resembles a line of surf on white sands, the man's fingers like inquisitive crabs. Jarius discovers a front hook and disables it. Cups slide away to either side with an almost imperceptible soft susurrus, disclosing proudly mounded prominences. Jarius's whiskered lips surround one gorging nipple, while his pinch cossets its sister.

Kerry's left hand scoops its partnered breast upward for its share of attention. She lifts drink from lap, blindly seeks a shelf, sidetable or sofa-arm, then lowers the glass onto air. The tumbler tumbles through space, landing with a splash of ice and liquid, feeding the thirsty carpet. Freed, her right hand cups the back of Jarius's neck

Her breasts accept minutes of languid suckling and stroking before she gapes her legs. Jarius quickly responds, sliding a slow hand up and down her nyloned flanks, moving higher with each zenith, pausing at the bare band below her loins. Kerry lifts her ass to free her skirt for the completion of the hoisting—then accidental, now intentional—begun when she first slid into the limo. Jarius cups her mounded cunt through the periwinkle fabric, and Kerry emits a soft mewl. Her hand traces the bulge of his cock through the cloth of his trousers.

Then, cessation of sensation. Kerry opens her eyes. Jarius stands some distance off, a desk drawer opening now to his fickle touch.

"Peter, what—"

Jarius's eyes seem to concentrate whatever dim light informs the room, twin furnace points. "Before we go any further, dearest, I'd like you to do something that would enhance my pleasure immeasurably. An easy thing, but rather titillating for both of us, I hope. Would you wear this?"

From the drawer, Jarius removes what seems at first a large floppy scrap of white leather. Then he displays it fully, like a proud salesman.

The calf-supple zippered bondage hood would look utterly familiar from a thousand common pornographic illusions, save for one odd feature: a stitch-edged irregular sinistral opening exactly contours Kerry's aubergine birthmark. Should she don this cowl, it would focus her silent, sometimes buried, never truly forgotten shame as if under an actinic spotlight.

Kerry gawps at the unexpected fetish garb, then nervously tugs her skirt down. "I won't. I don't feel right about it."

A MOUTHFUL OF TONGUES

Jarius slopes insinuatingly beside her on the couch, still offering the hood like some dark pope seeking to miter a new bishop. "Would you deny one of your own most salient charms, my dear? This innocent appurtenance merely serves to direct your lover's desire onto your uniquely erotic blemish. How often I've dreamed of caressing and kissing your maculate countenance, so ripe with nature's stain. You're like a bruised fruit demanding to be plucked. But hopefully you'll notice that even now, on the verge of our intimacy, I refrain until I receive your permission. Our first encounter must be perfect—"

Kerry's breasts are swaddled in blue lace again, and she's buttoning her jacket. "Mr. Jarius, I really have to leave now. Thank you for the dinner, and I'm sorry I let you get the wrong idea about us."

Jarius contemplates the virginal hood draping his deflating, still trousered erection. "I had this made just for you, Kerry."

Left boot won't accommodate her right foot. Kerry swaps stances, dons one waterproof shoe, then the other. "Can I get a ride home, Mr. Jarius? It's late, and the streets aren't safe."

Slumping, Jarius strokes the leather quietly for a few seconds, then bravely straightens and puts the cowl aside. "Our relationship is not at an end, Ms. Hackett. We'll discuss this further another day." The man rises to his feet and crosses to an intercom panel inset next to the door. He speaks orders quietly into the grille, then turns back to Kerry.

"Anselmo will be waiting with the car by the time you get downstairs."

Clutching her coat, Kerry darts out into the corridor.

With night's full descent, the echoing basement garage, its cement walls sweating gelidly, has become even chillier than earlier. Kerry hastens to enter the idling limo and declare her destination. For all the individual attention she receives from blank-faced Anselmo, she might as well be a cardboard box he's charged with delivering. Kerry stares blindly out the window until the short drive is over, as if mindlessly cataloging the city's manifold dispassionate obscenities. The purring limo pulls away from the curb in a cloud of frigid exhaust before she's even fully pushed past the unlatched outer door to her building. (The tiny lobby hosts no beggars.)

The small shadowy apartment at first appears empty of life, a crab's tenantless shell. A darkness-triggered nightlight in the galley kitchen valiantly spills an otiose radiance onto the vacant table. Expectedly missing is the NUfive bill Kerry pinned down almost twenty hours ago; but also gone are the six pill vials that anchored the cash.

"I sold the prescriptions on the street."

Tango's surly drunken voice emanates from a corner of the living-room containing his favorite chair, a lumpish flowery Goodwill piece, more hummock than furniture. Kerry crosses the familiar barely illuminated domestic terrain and sits on the broad chair arm. She lays a hand on Tango's coarse hair, brushing it off his forehead.

"You're already hot," she says quietly. "Why did you do it?"

Tango snorts. "Like you care? Coming in at this hour? Fuck, why not? I'll never be cured, not me or anyone else. They're just an expensive goddamn finger in the dike, those pills. Might as well start doing without them right now."

"You can't." Kerry's earnestly plaintive voice seems ready to break. "You have to go out right now and get them back from whoever you sold them to. You have to."

Tango thunders his reply. "I don't have to do *anything* you say, bitch!" Without warning, he shoves a thick hand up her skirt. "Didn't you even bring a change of panties, you little slut? He's dripping out of you."

"No, Tango, that's not true—"

Her waist is nearly encircled by Tango's disease-attenuated yet still strong paws. He immobilizes her while he erupts up from his seat. "I may be on the way out, but I can still remind you who you ought to be fucking!"

"Tango, don't—" Kerry tries to twist out of his pinioning, but can't. He lifts her struggling off her feet and carries her into the bedroom. Window blinds filter the streetlight into bars that slash the floor and furniture. He tosses her down onto the rumple-sheeted mattress, and quickly unzips himself.

Kerry's voice strive for reasonableness, but quavers uncontrollably. "We can make love, Tango, but you have to wear some protection, especially if you've gone a day without your medicine—"

"Fuck that. And I'm not dicking around where loverboy's already been."

Kerry frantically tries to lever herself up off the mattress. "No, Tango—"

He pushes her around and back down, onto her stomach. With one hand he wickets her neck, while with the other he strains aside the fabric of her underpants revealed by skirt's disarray. Kerry sobs wordlessly. He kneels astride her, bringing his hard cock into a bar of cold light: nubby welts like ceremonial scarring wrap his pellagric penis. He spits on his hand, transfers the saliva to his cicatriced cock, and brings its head to Kerry's asshole.

The man's wide glans pops through the tight muscled ring where earlier her dream jaguar's pointed cocktip only delicately snagged.

Tango's brutal strokes culminate after a blessedly brief set. He pulls out and retreats across the room. Kerry's quiet crying counterpoints the sound of his retoothing zipper.

"All right, now get out."

Kerry stifles her sobs. "What? You can't mean it—"

"Get out now, or I'll kick your ass out."

"Where will I go?"

"Back to loverboy."

"I can't. He's not—"

Tango swipes his arm across the top of her dresser, sending perfume phials and framed photos flying. "I said get lost! Or do you want to hang around until I can get it up again?"

Kerry regards the hunched, panting, disheveled figure for a long moment, her expression of disbelief segueing to one of grim acceptance. Then, with slow pained motions, she slides off the bed. One stocking clumps loosely around her calf. She makes no move to rummage in closet or bureau, but simply retrieves purse and coat, and sidles out the apartment without further imploring or lamentations, like a prisoner jailed for decades and now facing the long-imagined but unreally materialized end of her incarceration and the prospect of greeting an alien, unwelcoming world.

During her staircase descent, she pauses on a landing to fix her stockings. Adjusting them at her upper thigh, she pulls her hand back wetly rust-smeared. "Oh, Christ, not now." She rummages in her purse, finds a scuff-cased sanitary pad, unwraps it and clumsily layers it into place at her crotch, heedless of her semi-public exposure.

Again, no friendly beggar graces the ground-floor vestibule. Kerry steps out onto the empty sidewalk. Pulling her thin coat more tightly about her, she walks away from her violated lost home.

Halfway toward her only possible destination, she spies a lone soldier at the same moment he catches sight of her. She stops and stands in an unthreatening posture, hands well away from her pockets. The soldier advances quickly, rifle held at the ready.

A lithe young black man, he wears his fatigues and equipment awkwardly, as if newly conscripted. Beneath the brim of his helmet, his features summon the image of a chiseled pagan icon, somatic planes of burnished tropical lumbers. A patch across his breast proclaims him PVT. SHANGOLD.

Unmoving, Kerry shivers against the encroaching chill. "I have my ID in my purse—"

"Shut up. Come with me."

"Why? Wait a minute—where's your partner?"

The soldier hooks her arm. "I said shut up!" He yanks her forward, and Kerry is forced to stumble ahead of him. Only a few dozen steps separate them from the maw of a dark alley. Propelled within that dank, fetid channel, Kerry pitches boomingly against a big metal dumpster. Strap snapping, her purse tumbles away. When she turns, the soldier has slung his weapon across his back.

"Kneel down."

"No, don't—"

The soldier clamps hands atop her shoulders and forces her to her knees. Grit bites her nyloned knees, and the toes of her shoes scrape twin troughs in the alley's debris. Transferring a clawlike grip to the short hair feathering her nape, the rogue soldier cants Kerry's face to within a few inches of his trousers. He unsnaps his waistband fastening and drags down his zipper. He wears no briefs, and his hair-nested unclipped cock sags atop plummy wrinkled balls. A blunt thumb lofts his meat toward her mouth, while two fingers of the same hand pry between her lips, nails scraping teeth.

Kerry reluctantly allows her mouth to be pried open, and the soldier's cock communions her tongue. Her mouth's hot moisture catalyzes the growth of his dick, and it burgeons swiftly between her lips. Puppetting her head while he rocks his hips back and forth, the black man fucks her mouth with growing intensity.

Kerry's eyes are closed, and she perforce supports herself against the soldier's hairy thighs. Gutteral groans escape him, and an accelerating tempo betrays his impending climax.

At the last instant, he pulls entirely out. Kerry partially averts her face, and he pumps his fragrant jism across the gap between them to splash athwart her birthmark: silver lakes clump that wine-dark continent, mercury flecks the forest of her lashes.

As Kerry raises a hand to her smirched face, something cuts the air above her head. There sounds a concussive thump, inanimate material connecting with flesh and bone, and then the soldier is crumpled across the alley floor.

Kerry clumsily gathers her feet beneath her, stands and faces the dumpster.

Half-revealed in the open vertical trash door, like Punch in a pantomime, stands the beggar who haunts her building. Leering gap-toothedly, he clutches a bent length of pipe, its threaded business end blackened with blood.

"Better run, lady. Better run."

Her hand is still trembling when she places it on the security scanner in the atrium of the Diaverde building. Ensconced in their impregnable synthetic transparent turret, the brace of clean-cut night guards watch her suspiciously; even recognizing her, they are plainly distrustful of her dirty, disarrayed, purseless state. When the elevator acknowledges her and invites her onboard, the sentinels minimally relax.

Empty at this hour of even the most dedicated researcher, the tenth floor casts back the noise of her footsteps as if her spectral double walks beside her. The second scanner at the entrance to Project Benthos responds with alacrity to her tentative palm-caress.

Lights brighten automatically as the door swings shut behind her. At the control panel visited earlier, Kerry fingers the sequence of commands Dr. Teague used to summon the benthic from its homeostatic environment. Within a minute, the trolley-borne aquarium rests on the far side of the glass partition within reach of the manipulator gloves.

The limber acrobatic benthic adheres to some non-diurnal schedule, as active nocturnally as during the day. Perhaps it never needs to rest, engineered reservoirs of barely contained energy continuously propelling its silky furlings and beckoning flagellations, its coy curlings and enticing involutions around the clock.

Kerry tears her eyes away from the exogamically desirable creature, totipotent sovereign in its small realm, and steps to a workbench. Neatly racked tools yield a sharp blade. Knife pinched between thumb and forefinger of her right hand, she inserts her weapon into one metal-cuffed work glove. The blade sinks easily into the index fingertip of the glove, catches in the dense rubber, responds to Kerry's increased pressure, emerges questingly into the segregated air beyond the glass. A warning light reddens the control board. She torques the blade, enlarging the hole, then withdraws the instrument and tosses it to the floor. She thrusts her hand into the damaged glove, which comes assistingly alive. She lifts the hinged lid of the container, and dips her gashed finger into the waters of the tank.

Instantly alert and eager as any lover, the ultraresponsive benthic compresses itself to threadlike dimensions and flows into the mutilated glovetip like a finely knitted lace shawl slipped through a wedding ring.

Before Kerry can even withdraw her hand from within its partial rubber casing, the benthic has propulsively coursed the thruway of her arm, mucigenously alive against her flesh beneath her clothing. She stumbles back several paces, leaving the servomotors of the now-empty glove to whine down to silence.

A broad glistening coral-tinged pseudopod of the benthic pops up from beneath her shirtcollar, rearing back like a hooded snake calculatedly considering where to strike. At the same instant Kerry involuntarily opens her mouth, gasps, and clamps a hand to her invaded crotch.

A portion of the upper hovering element of the benthic darts down her throat, reversing the magician's common trick of pulling silken scarf from gullet. Extrusions splay across her alarmed countenance, infiltrating eyes, ears and nostrils like needles of wind.

A MOUTHFUL OF TONGUES

Kerry collapses to the floor, dorsal side down, her face suddenly eerily composed beneath the benthic's gaudy film.

Now begins Kerry Hackett's transubstantiation, a conversion of flesh to more than flesh, a seachange of self.

Kerry's clothing commences slowly to dissolve, as if eaten by an esurient acid from beneath. But the liquefied raw materials of her garments do not pool away to the floor or sublimate into the air; instead, they are greedily absorbed directly into her newly hyperporous skin. Rejected metal fittings fall away, clinking to the tiles. Her mother's thin gold chain bursts from expansive pressures and slips off her neck, puddling on the floor like a patch of jungle sunlight.

Naked now, Kerry's supine body exhibits no activity for a short eternity. Then, convulsive tremors surge across her from toes to scalp. Her body flattens and spreads unnaturally, like an air bag simultaneously melting and deflating; imploding, her facial features vanish inward, as do her breasts. Her short black hair is reeled inside her. Arms merge into torso, legs fuse, as the forked stick of her humanity backward eggs. Livid waves of organically hued colors race each other across this ovoid corporeal landscape.

The lab clock parcels out an hour as the Kerry-larva merely intelligently pullulates. Waves of metabolic heat rising off the autocatalyzing protoplasmic mound trigger the lab's air-conditioning to new activity.

The next stage of totipotent-directed evolution manifests first as fractally distributed ripples, as if a complex net beneath the grub's epidermis were being shaken from multiple points. Then, reprogramming and redefinition: from distal loci, perfect digits emerge, tender pink toes and fingers with nails already tinted a unique scarab green. Limbs separate away, resuming their identity, tendons and muscles flexing. At crux of legs, mons and cunt resurface, complete with a slow trickle of menstrual blood filtering through the labia. Ribs recage themselves, a navel invaginates, breasts bud and swell, crowning themselves with nipples. Hair rethatches skull, ears appear, and the Kerry-physiognomy, that unique assemblage of cartilage, jelly, muscle and bone, pushes out from inside like an image formed from behind in a toy composed of a million floating microscopic pins.

Perfect from toenails to teeth, breathing deeply, the nude Kerry Hackett lies on the cold tiles. Only one visible difference distinguishes her reinvigorated body from her former shell:

Her birthmark is missing from her immaculate face, sluiced off like so much maquillage.

Kerry's eyes snap open without warning flutter. Brimming with novel internal and external perceptions, they convey a kind of alien humor abetted by her serene sly smile. Effortlessly, disdaining use of her hands, she vaults to her feet with only a subtle twitch of her leg musculature.

A wallhook surrenders its short lab coat. Wrapped in virginal white, unshod, bare-legged, Kerry reaches the lab door and slides through.

Two guards sit relaxed in their groundfloor booth, talking.

"Who're our replacements today?"

"Maureen and Isaiah."

"They should be here any minute."

Kerry's appearance startles the bored watchers: barefoot, barely clad, radiating a kind of abnormal, seductive vitality. One guard triggers their intercom.

"Can we help you, ma'am?"

Kerry opens her coat, revealing her shining allure, the pitcher-plant perfection of her reworked body. She flattens herself against their booth, breasts mashing distortedly, and squirms as if in heat.

"She's high on something. We should stop her before she hurts herself."

The flick of a switch unseals the unbreachable booth. One man emerges. Kerry hurls herself amorously into his arms. Unprepared, the guard reacts with a slow defensiveness. Kerry has time to plaster her lips against his. His eyes widen, he gags, and his legs buckle.

The fallen guard's partner has a hand on his holstered gun. Kerry steps into the booth with him.

"Hold it right there, lady—"

Kerry smiles, and protrudes the tip of her tongue as if lasciviously to lick her lips. But her drupleted strawberry tongue fails to continue its betokened motion, instead muscling itself forward, hauling its own animated substance easily onto the ledge of Kerry's lower jaw, the gobbet of stropping, vocable muscle plainly autonomous and impossibly severed from its roots, poising there like a miniscule predator, toad or lizard, before launching itself across the gap and splatting against the guard's face. The tongue swims down his scream, and he instantly loses consciousness.

Her motions economic and swift, Kerry strips the shoes and uniform from one of the guards. Lower legs into the narrow pants, she finds them difficult to pull up over her hips. With a small kind of shrug or wriggle, redistributing her mass, her hips instantly accommodate themselves to the requisite dimensions. Dressed in her plausible disguise, Kerry leaves the building before the new guards arrive.

A few early workers move through the dawn-rumored streets. Kerry strides boldly, looking about her with evident fresh-eyed pleasure. Some blocks away from the Diaverde buildings, she stops before the window of a travel agency.

A poster depicts a tropical scene: golden beach with sunbathers, palms shading a drinkbar, sailboats asurf. (In fringing jungle, does a feline face hide?) The poster bears a legend, and, her replacement tongue languorously traversing palate and tapping teeth, Kerry pronounces the invitation aloud:

"Come to Bahia."

The guard's wallet offers a Metro card with plenty of stripe credit to buy her a ticket on the hourly shuttle to the airport.

In the main terminal, threading among the rifle-bearing soldiers, Kerry heads directly to the nearest woman's toilet. This early, the lavatory features few users. Minutes pass before a petite red-haired Hispanic woman clad in a floral-print dress enters, trundling a suitcase on wheels. Kerry smiles, and the woman returns the friendly security guard's expression.

"Would you watch this for me?"

"Sure."

The woman opens a stall door, is startled to find Kerry right behind her.

"What's wrong?"

"Nothing."

Kerry pushes the woman inside the stall, and seals her cries with a thick kiss. Swallowing Kerry's third tongue, the woman drops. Kerry arranges her on the toilet, and begins to undress her victim. At the same time, she is dissolving the guard's uniform, this time allowing the degenerate materials to slip down the stall's floor drain. But Kerry continues to shed quarts of cloudy liquid mass beyond the weight of the clothing, shrinking and morphing in rippling cascades until she wears the exact appearance of the unconscious woman.

Dressed in new clothes, in charge of her victim's purse and luggage, Kerry proceeds to a Web kiosk and purchases her ticket to Bahia online, using the small woman's credit card.

Boarding time arrives. The exit official hands Kerry's adopted passport back to her. "Have a safe flight, Ms. Yemana."

"I'm sure I will."

Aloft, Kerry relaxes in her comfortable first-class seat. The plane's circulatory system murmurs. Stewards circulate with food and refreshing beverages. Out the window, clouds part to reveal acres of indivisible ocean, beneath which incredible creatures swim, their rich lives a communal secret. Kerry rubs the fabric cushion of her seat, smiles, raises her glass of ice-soothed liquor, and allows the tip of her fourth tongue—for the moment, firmly rooted—to curl droplets of the drink into her mouth like a cat's. She closes her eyes, and the fabric of her cushion coarsens beneath her touch. She is seated on a piece of burlap folded across the wooden bench of a lumbering rattling bus. A hot urban wind enters the open frame at her elbow. Outside the window, shacks fester under a brilliant sun. Her fellow passengers are tropic-bred and poverty-clad, chattering in a foreign language. Kerry closes her eyes again, stroking the burlap. The mule's rough hair divides beneath her touch, tickling. Her legs barrel its ribbed solidity. Kerry holds reins, but her mule is being led by another rider, down a rutted unpaved road hemmed in by dense foliage. A cool breeze carries exotic scents from the jungle. Buildings thrust up around her, and she alights from a small carriage. She strides confidently across cobbles, onto a granite-slabbed sidewalk and through the hotel door. A console radio big as a Web server (Web server?) is playing rollicking carnival tunes.

Kerry steps to the front desk, where a clerk says something unintelligible. A robust, middle-aged man, his black mustache thick as a broom, he bears one empty striped sleeve, folded and pinned to itself. Smiling, he offers her what is obviously his name—"Senhor Arlindo Quincas" —and plainly asks for hers. Smiling brightly, remaining unspeaking, Kerry touches the man's sweaty arm, sucking beads of his perspiration through her fingertips. Pleased by the touch of this small dark sexy woman, he returns her smile, and continues to speak. In a minute, his words come into focus for her:

"—welcome, Senhorita. Welcome to Bahia."

PART TWO

Around the entire columned perimeter of the broad white-painted veranda that wrapped three sides of the Blue Afternoon Hotel, save where interrupted by flights of street-seeking blue-washed steps on east, south and west (along the north wall, fence-shielded from passersby, only trash canisters, slop pails, discarded furniture, broken pottery), grew an assortment of tall shrubs, leaves like green thumbprints, their riotous vitality barely constrained by the day-to-day efforts of a shabby-hatted, mahogany-faced Dartpipe gardener currently trimming at them in the heat of midday with an irregularly langorous snick-snick of his long-handled shears. Anchored in the rich soil with strong roots like the arthritic hands of wooden giants, the foliage filtered the gentle Bahian sea-breezes that blessed the hotel and its guests, adding overscents reminiscent of creosote, eucalyptus and rosemary to the marine-tinged wind.

Adjacent to the main entrance of the hotel, where they could be assured of full visual inspection of the passing parade of citizens, tradesmen, employees and guests, a group of local men idled in high-backed wicker chairs clustered around a glass-topped table set on wrought-iron legs. Their skin tones ranged naturally from milk-pale to loam-dark, but they shared the same easy demeanor. The collars of colorfully patterned barkcloth shirts vee'd at their necks; linen trousers in various shades of grey, tan, flea and dusty mauve draped their insouciantly crossed legs; woven sandals cradled broad unsocked, thick-nailed feet. The drinking hand of each man firmly clasped a tall glass filled with an emerald concoction of potent guava liqueur, shaved ice, and pineapple juice; a condensation-beaded pitcher of the same mix centered the table. The less-favored hand of each man flounced a cambric handkerchief, fancifully embroidered with its owner's initials by lover or wife, sister or mother, aunt or grandmother. Frequently the men sopped their sweat-birthing brows as they sipped.

People came and went past the ostensibly disinterested yet unflagging audience of five idlers. Breezes romped like lazy kittens. Glasses were drained and refilled. Then a skinny, gnarl-jointed man with eyes cupped in deep orbits spoke:

"One hears that Senhor Arlindo Quincas keeps a woman now, right here in the hotel."

A distinguished older man, silver chest hairs sprinkled among his black thicket, replied, "Such a scandal is fast becoming common knowledge."

"She is a foreigner," eagerly offered a third fellow, fresh-faced and younger than all his comrades. "She arrived here without so much as a quill or scale or claw to her name. Unable to pay her bill after her first week, she persuaded Quincas to settle her debt in other coinage."

Knowing masculine smiles tweaked their lips. A fourth man, round as a bladder full of rubber sap, asked, "Has anyone seen her?"

"No, she stays in her room."

The youngest man said, "I have heard she bleeds without stopping."

"In the manner of a woman during her menses?"

"Apparently. For over a week."

"Is she sick?"

"Not that I have heard. Quincas takes his pleasure without regard to her condition anyway."

"Perhaps he makes use of alternate routes."

"Perhaps."

The fat man said, "There is also the matter of her meals."

"Her meals? What of them?"

"They are inordinately large. Even I would have trouble finishing them. Yet her tray returns to the kitchen three times a day, cleaned to the last gravy splatter."

The men sat silently, pondering these piquant life-broadening mysteries. After a time a ferret-faced fellow, unspeaking till now, asked with oily obsequious-ness, "Does the honorable Senhor Reymoa know of all this?"

A sour expression from the gaunt man greeted mention of the Reymoa name. "Is there anything in this town—material or immaterial—that escapes the greedy clutches of Ovid Reymoa? It seems he must own everything, whether tangible or not. And whatever the old man himself does not discover and claim, his busybody, avaricious sons pick up."

The senior member of the idlers said, "Wastrels both. At least Ovid earned his wealth. But his sons— I am not sure which one I despise more, Hermeto or Getulio."

"I would prefer either to the daughter."

"I also. Darciana is the more reprehensible, for concealing such a vile nature in such an attractive package."

Silence recurred, as the idlers seemed to ponder with deep disquiet the Reymoa brood. Finally, returning to their original topic, the distinguished man offered a last item for consideration:

"I have heard that, despite not enjoying the deep distinction of being born in Bahia, the mistress of Quincas nonetheless speaks our language impeccably."

"Ah!" "A faculty in her favor!" "So few foreigners honor our noble tongue!" "This obviates much!"

Satisfied with having accorded this suspect member of the fairer sex at least one due honor, the idlers sat back with their cool drinks and soft stitched napery to enjoy the waning day until their various evening assignations—dinner, theater, tryst, night-fishing or sleep—called them away.

* * *

Varnished joinery from long-vanished craftsmanly hands, rust-flecked foliate hinges, bronze numerals, faceted glass handle. A faint musty scent blocked by the wooden barrier vying with the stronger odors of floor polish, lavender sachets and insecticides.

Outside the door to Room 334, Arlindo Quincas paused. With his lone hand, he tugged the empty pinned sleeve of his crisp shirt into a configuration more dapper, then smoothed back his pomade-slicked hair and, fingers now carrying away a trace of clear gel, combed fragrant oils upon his hedge-thick mustache. Quiet and unpeopled at this hot midafternoon hour, the shadowy hotel hall seemed to stretch away from the unassuming door infinitely in both directions, the hall's threadbare figured blue runner assuming the likeness of a river without source or outlet. Eyeleted ivory curtains framing open unscreened windows stirred gently in the iodined breeze from the sea.

Grooming complete, Quincas rather timorously knocked. A woman's voice called out firmly, "Enter, Arlindo." At the sound of his own name, Quincas took a deep breath, as if to master some rogue emotion. His knuckles whitened when he gripped the door handle. He opened the door and stepped through into the room.

He shut the door behind him, but did not advance much beyond the threshold.

Artificial twilight suffused the rococo chamber like a ghostly spiced phoenix-nest of smoky threads. A lurid empire, Senhorita Yemana lay naked across her bed, a small wad of towels stuffed between her legs. Her sumptuous form athwart the creased sheets drew Quincas's concentrated attention as a well swallows a bucket.

In her face alone did she resemble the woman who had checked into his hotel nine days ago, touching Quincas so intimately on the arm and thus precipitating many unanticipatable events. Otherwise, she was a different woman entirely. Her formerly dark-skinned, petite body had altered to a white-skinned, fuller-fleshed one, and she stretched now at least six inches taller. Her auburn hair too had undergone a transformation, mysteriously losing its waves and darkening. And she must have cut it—though Quincas had been unable to find scissors or discarded snippage.

A small lizard, tangerine striped with lemon, crossed the wall above the headboard. The noise of its claws and pads on the wallpaper was discernible as a skittish scratching.

"How have you passed the day?" Quincas asked tentatively, breaking the silence.

Fingers interlaced to cushion further her down-pillowed head, arms bent with elbows aimed ceilingward, showing her axillary thatch, Senhorita Yemana smiled and, with a nearly imperceptible muscular effort, released languorous ophidian ripples throughout her breasts, torso and legs.

"As usual, Arlindo. Learning to know myself."

Quincas coughed politely. "The philosophers claim that such a course of study generally occupies the whole length of our lives."

"Oh, no, I am quite finished today."

Quincas had no reply ready for this uncommon assertion. Instead, he wrinkled his nose. "Forgive me, but this room smells like an ill-kept lion cage at the zoo. Will you give me leave to dispose of your soiled sanitary rags, or do you still persist in accumulating them?"

"There is no cause to worry. I am done bleeding now. The need for such spillage no longer exists within me." Senhorita Yemana sat up, breasts swaying like hammocked melons, and dug the encarnadined cloths from the warm repository of her crotch. She cupped the sodden mass of fabric in her hands for a moment, as if molding clay, then loosed a froth-netted wad of saliva into it. She turned on her side briefly and dropped the newest rags onto the others that had accumulated there between bed and wall.

Quincas crossed himself and whispered a name of pagan comfort. "I fail to see how that happy fact alters the need to dispose of the unwholesome refuse."

"Do not trouble yourself with the matter, Arlindo. Come here. Now you can finally have my cunt. Unless you have grown to prefer my mouth?"

The man's limbs trembled, and he stammered. Sweat broke from his brow in the warm stuffy room. "I—I cannot—"

"Cannot choose? No, of course not. Yet why should you have to? Approach me now."

Quincas advanced unsteadily, until the knees of his trousers brushed the mattress. Already, his maximally engorged cock strained painfully against the single layer of fabric and buttons interfering with its newly attuned pleasure. Senhorita Yemana's uncannily nimble fingers quickly unbuttoned him. His trousers pooled around his ankles, and he stepped from them, shoes dragging hems. Coarse-haired muscular thighs pedestaled the sizable trophy of his disclosed manhood.

The woman palmed his penis one-handedly: glans resting on her blue-capillaried wrist, her fingers reached only two-thirds of the way to its root. Quincas closed his eyes with a self-protective caution made familiar over the past week.

Shifting closer in her sitting position, the woman brought her moistly parted lips to within several inches of Quincas's cockhead. Inside her mouth, her conventionally positioned and shaped tongue bloomed into strangeness.

Her tongue uncoiled outward into the air like the sentient spathe of some undiscovered plant. The velveteen instrument, stippled ruby and rose brocade, lofted above Quincas's cock momentarily, then dropped atop it. With his glans just kissing her bottom lip, his entire cock was mantled with her tongue, the underside of his dick yet bare, now that the woman had unpalmed him.

Then, without other movement, the Senhorita's tongue extended itself along its width, circling the draped cock. Meeting beneath, the edges of the tongue fused, enclosing Quincas's cock in a tight articulated tube.

Quincas released a solemn moan. The woman grabbed his buttocks and drew him forward by the leash of his tongue-sheathed cock.

In the shortest possible time, her face nested against his stomach and pubic hair, nose denting his belly, open lips pressed against his flesh, entubated cock concealed down her throat.

This fellatristic tableau exhibited no exterior movement: no head-bobbing, no sliding lips, no assistance of hand-stroking, no pumping of the man's grip-immobilized hips. Nonetheless, Quincas's sweaty shut-eyed face swiftly revealed the existence and progress of a secret agitation. His lower jaw slipped, the better to let groans and gruntings escape. He laid his hands atop the Senhorita's unshifting head, but could contribute no direction to her hidden tubal milking of his dick.

In less than a minute, Quincas bucked and climaxed. Senhorita Yemana remained fixed as a remora until his last spasms ceased. Then she pulled back her head, smiling with dripless lips, and, with a tongue conforming to the human norm, said, "Now lie on the bed."

Quincas's eyes opened, even as his knees jellied. "But I cannot rise up again so soon—"

"Do what I say."

A MOUTHFUL OF TONGUES

Quincas climbed on the bed and lay on his back. The woman straddled him, reached behind herself to clench his not-yet-quite-unstiffened cock, and guided it inside her osculatory cunt. She sank down to what appeared their mutual limits of mating. But then, without any impetus from Quincas, his hips jerked upward to effect an even deeper socketing. Even his balls rose up and half out of sight. He shifted to brace himself in this difficult but not-impossible position.

Her unnatural cunt, like matched mouth, began to work without gross motions of the attached body, all devious pulsations and slippage occuring invisibly within.

During this encounter, whether from natural male limits or induced prolongation, Quincas's orgasm was longer in coming. Minutes passed as the man ecstatically succumbed to the woman above him, eyes again closed, his face deformed with pleasure. Senhorita Yemana's expression betokened a lesser yet real joy.

Midway through the static extraction of Quincas's second burden of cum, Senhorita Yemana looked toward the narrow gap between bed and wall, drawn by the delicate approach of the iridescent lizard across the wallpaper. The tiny reptile seemed attracted by some movement below her line of sight.

What seemed a child's blunt bandaged hand, the wrappings spotted with blood and other straw-colored internal seepages, emerged to grip the mattress edge. A second followed. The hands pulled the rest of the entity up into view:

Formed of Senhorita Yemana's discarded, cohering, entwined and ennervated menstrual rags, the creature resembled a small mummy or generally featureless papier-mache humanoid. Standing atop the mattress, it seemed to regard its mother with a fond curiosity, its lack of eyes no hindrance to its affection.

Continuing her ministrations upon the pleasure-rapt, pleasure-blinded Quincas, the woman reached out to bestow a tender brush of her fingers upon the ragchild's cheek.

"Go now," she whispered to it.

The ragchild stepped around the oddly unrocking fucking couple; but in doing so, it trailed a gauze foot across Quincas's leg.

"What is that?" asked Quincas in alarm.

Senhorita Yemana shielded his opening eyes. "Nothing. A fly. Can you feel me do this new thing?"

Quincas suddenly gasped. "What have you done?"

"Just a small teasing root down into your cock. Relax."

Quincas gave in. The ragchild now stood at the door to the hall. It leaped up to grab the handle, turned it and swung the door open a crack with its small inertia. Releasing its grip, it scampered out of the room.

When Quincas came, he howled like an ox-gored wolf.

The woman climbed off both the man and the bed. No fluids seeped from her cunt. She began to dress in the new clothes Quincas had purchased to accommodate her altered dimensions.

After a time Quincas spoke, calmly, earnestly, but without any real hope.

"I have no wife, nor any close relations. My livelihood is assured, and my earnings more than enough for us both. Would you stay with me yet for some time—for as long as you desire?"

Tying her long orchid-printed wrap of a skirt, she presented her back to the supine man. When she turned, she wore an Anglo face he had never seen, half-clouded with a blazing burgundy birthmark. "No, Arlindo. I have to move on. It is my nature."

Quincas began unashamedly to cry. The woman with the stranger's face walked over to him and began to undo his shirt. She pulled it away from the stump of his arm. "There is one final favor I will grant you, for your kindness."

She leaned over, her breasts wallowing on his chest, and began to larrup his time-smoothed stump with her slightly swollen tongue. Quincas said bewilderedly through his tears, "It tingles."

"It should." Finished with the slow application of her saliva, she moved away and resumed dressing, high-laced sandals and a lilac cotton blouse.

At the door, the woman paused. The room's third occupant, the lizard, clung to the jamb, seemingly intent on following Senhorita Yemana out. Quicker than the snuffling Quincas could blink, she plucked the crawler off by the tail. The creature hung untwitching, with an odd indifference to its capture

A MOUTHFUL OF TONGUES

"Put aside your silly disappointment, Arlindo. You cannot know me well enough to realize how foolish a request I am denying."

The lizard disappeared somewhere, and then so did the woman.

* * *

When Arlindo Quincas appeared among the five veranda-ensconced idlers with his brawny new arm, a perfect match down to the patterned swirls of hair for its older, everyday companion, their reactions were suitably dramatic and their astonished encomiums agreeably heartfelt. In his fresh short-sleeved white shirt from Veloso's Dry Goods, Quincas allowed the five men to press and palpitate his new appendage, poke and prod and flex it like a whole churchful of Doubting Thomases.

"Modern medical science will have to be revised in its entirety," the senior member of the group declaimed authoritatively after all had satisified themselves of the integrity of Quincas's restored arm. The leader of the idlers wiped sweat from his Roman nose and raised his glass. "A salute!" Several rounds of drinks followed, necessitating delivery of a new pitcher from the bar by a doe-eyed Dartpipe girl in hotel livery, who bore also a tray of roasted kinkajou snacks. (Accompanied by a mysterious, sourceless, nearly subliminal castanet-like clicking, this lithe young india carried herself with quiet dignity.)

Finishing a mouthful of meat tugged from its skewer, the distinguished gentleman said, "I propose we mount a delegation to Doctor Flávio Zefiro this very afternoon."

Protectively cradling his new arm with the other, Quincas vetoed the proposal. "No, no, I have no wish to spend the rest of my life in examining rooms and lecture halls. I refuse to make a grand production of this private miracle."

Their emaciated compatriot, his obtrusive Adam's-apple bobbing, announced, "We could not see the doctor today anyway. His horse and carriage are gone, and I have heard he visits the capitol in order to resupply his pharmacy."

For his part, the youngest man seemed unwilling to let the matter drop. "But how can you keep such a wonderful occurrence from your admiring fellow citizens? People are bound to talk."

"Let them talk. I will deny everything. The accident at the cane mill never took place. Who remembers the events of fifteen years ago anyway? Memory is a trickster. I myself find even my recent memories cloudy. Who can say for sure if I ever once entertained a foreign woman of easy virtue and uncanny powers within the walls of The Blue Afternoon? Although my chimerical lover has been gone for only two days, it seems a lifetime has passed. Confined to my bed with a fever for that whole first day, I lost all sense of place and self for hours at a stretch."

The rotund man stroked his own wattles pensively and said, "And yet you claim your appetite was still keen?"

Quincas nodded. "I chewed and swallowed efficiently, although as in a dream."

The shifty-featured fellow now interrupted. "Have you considered the financial angle?" He rubbed the large mole anchoring his nose with sly meaning and said, "People would pay considerable fees to witness your regenerated limb and hear your tale."

Waving away the suggestion, Quincas reaffirmed his intentions. "Never. That would be a blasphemy on her memory and what she did for me."

The angular, haunted-eyed idler who had known of Doctor Flávio Zefiro's journey snorted and said, "Blasphemy indeed! Why, some of the hints you have let slip about this Lilith lead me to believe the blasphemy has already taken place."

Quincas curled his new hand into a fist. "There are some properties of my restored muscles I have yet to test."

The silver-haired spokesman intervened with soothing words, and soon all six men were companionably drinking their green cocktails.

Steadily approaching throughout this conversation had been the noise of the snacking blades of the Dartpipe gardener. Now from the far side of the foliage directly adjacent to the idlers' table arose a thick rope of herbal smoke. Seeing this token of his longtime employee, Quincas spoke in a jovial tone that owed as much to alcohol as to his miracle cure. "Why, even the 'pipes, with all their superstitions, accept my good luck without carping questions. Let me show you. Ixay! Come up here a moment!"

The gardener ascended the nearest steps and approached the seated men. He doffed his dusty, abused hat, but continued to puff on his rootlike hand-plaited cigar. His dark seamed face, a board with knotholes for eyes, revealed no emotions.

"Ixay, what do you and the other indios say about my new arm?"

The gardener removed his cigar, exhaled a final mushroom of smoke, then replied with calm consideration, "You have met a very powerful bruja, treated her kindly, and benefited thereby. There is nothing unusual in this. My own father knew a witch woman who could live underwater for days at a time, her mother having been a manatee, and once for him she located a knife dropped overboard during a fishing expedition. But of course, not everyone who encounters *your* woman may be so fortunate. May I return to my work now?"

"Yes, yes, go."

The idlers and the hotel-keeper pondered the indio's speech for an interval. Then the youngest man, fingering his wispy blonde goatee in a meditative manner, said, "Is the bruja whom Arlindo kept still resident in Bahia? I wonder. Indeed, I do."

* * *

The shack nestled in a grove of towering trees with leaves like glossy straps, each tree sovereign of a large sphere of territory in which other growths were arboreally discouraged from taking root, so that the overall effect within the grove was that of an almost engineered, green-canopied clearing with a hard-dirt floor intermittently staked with massive ridged trunks resembling curvilinear stacks of wooden rings. The trees harbored much wildlife, however: chittering monkeys, chattering parrots, chirping songbirds. A large striped bird with a beak like maladjusted pliers lived on the oily cueball-sized nuts produced by the trees, littering the clearing floor with bits of husks, a raffia rain. Slow lemurs, silent as nuns and precise as accountants, moved wide-eyed through the canopy. Regal lizards conspired atop a lone outcropping of shale, reptile aristocrats manning an undefeated Bastille. Butterfly divas sipped at the flagons of orchids of a thousand colorations and designs, the only other plant privileged by the trees to share their realm, hanging in tangles at various heights like irregular curtains in a faerie theater.

Built haphazardly of scavenged materials—ragged planks, mismatched beams—the small shack appeared unlikely to be divided into more than a single room. From the upper corner of the roof—shingled with thick slabs of hirsute bark; slanting downward back to front—a tin stovepipe poked toward the patchwork sky (unscribbled by clouds or contrails, bleached at zenith by imperial sun). No windows interrupted the hut's walls, and its door, taken from some inappropriately elegant structure, overlapped its allotted opening on two sides, while gaping on two others; held in place with lashings of mariner's rope, its dragging corner had scored an arclike trench in the clearing floor.

A rough path led out of the clearing toward the east. Down this trail now, returning to the clearing, trudged a lone figure.

Strapped to the back of the thin, androgynous, bare-foot and drably shift-clad hiker was a canvas-topped wicker basket almost taller than its bearer. The adolescent struggling beneath the pack showed the mixed facial features of a mestiza beneath bowl-cut jet hair: rusty complexion, eyes the color of damp alluvial soil, unsplayed nose, thin lips. The mestiza's ears were pierced and sported half a dozen cheap earrings of hammered copper and colored glass.

In front of the closed door to the shack, the mestiza unshucked her pannier with an awkward shrug of relief. She kneaded her lower back for a moment, arching into her knuckles. Then, her brief moment of rest over, she knocked tentatively on the door and called out, "Senhor Lazaro, are you awake? I am back with our supplies."

No answer. The young woman refrained from opening the door or calling a second time. Animals rustled above her, secure in their duties, and a blob of sunlight crawled an infinitesimal distance across her toes. She placed her fingers atop the taut drawstring-cinched canvas covering the pannier and softly drummed a popular tune she had heard in the city.

A MOUTHFUL OF TONGUES

After five minutes there came a sequence of noises from within the shack: the creak of a rope-strung bed, unintelligible muttering, the clink of bottle on glass, the hearty smacking of lips, a grunt—and then a startling crash and bang, followed by loud cursing.

"Goddamn this unholy broom! Who left this broom here! Caozinha! If you are back, what are you doing waiting outside like some specter! Get in here, goddamn you!"

Caozinha ceased her near-silent drumming, sighed, and then tugged open the door, digging the trench a little deeper.

Lit by a struggling kerosene lantern, the shadowed interior of the shack resembled a diorama compiled by two competing curators: a self-taught naturalist intent on exhibiting a troglodyte's simple life and a do-gooding reformer hoping to provide an educational illustration for his text on Bahian poverty. Rude tools—a mattock, a saw, a dibble—occupied one corner; a narrow bed with wafer-thin mattress and bunched coverlets hulked against one wall; a sheet-metal stove supplied the roof's pipe; a rickety castoff table—helpfully supported from total collapse by two rock-solid chairs assembled from unshaven logs—offered a precarious perch to a bottle of clear liquor and a pottery mug; canted shelves bore various victuals in bins, boxes, jars and cans. The offending broom had been kicked under the bed.

But the irresistible focus of the room was the giant man who staggered now across the creaking floorboards, blinking olivine eyes against the daylight. He wore only a pair of stained white shorts such as a fisherman might favor, the rest of his light-skinned lardy flesh-acreage sown with a rich crop of bronze curling hair. His elf-knotted beard reached halfway to his cannonball gut, an ersatz pregnancy; his hands, cupped, would have concealed a good portion of Caozinha's head.

"Move your skinny tail," Lazaro demanded. Caozinha responded quickly, wrestling the pannier inside. By the time she had closed the door upon them, sealing man and girl away from the happy sunlight as in a crypt, Lazaro had already seated himself on a sturdy chair and poured himself a second drink.

"You lingered too long in town," he said after swallowing a slug of liquor.

"No, I most certainly did not. I completed our business with all dispatch. And in fact, I hurried back, because once I entered the forest, I sensed something following me."

"Something? What kind of something?"

"I do not know. I never saw it fully. From the noises and my glimpses of it, it seemed the size of a child. But it moved like a wild animal."

Lazaro finished his drink so hastily that half slopped out to bedew his dirty beard. "What foolishness! It was probably one of the boys your own age from the town. He hoped to persuade you to fuck him, because everyone there knows what a slut you are."

Caozinha only replied, "I have to put away our purchases."

"And where is the change?"

"There is no change! Not a quill! I had to bargain like a Jew to stretch our money as far as I did."

Lazaro snorted. "Hurry up then."

Caozinha did not dawdle, but neither did she move speedily. Lazaro continued to drink, while watching her raptorishly. Midway through her sorting of their provisions, Lazaro asked her, "What were people talking of in town? What gossip did you acquire?"

Caozinha paused. "Nothing. Nothing unusual has occurred since I was there last."

Lazaro nodded, as if hearing once more of the town's bland and somnolent facade fulfilled his cynical expectations.

Although she moved with all permissible deliberation, Caozinha had to finish her chore eventually. She hung the wicker backpack from a peg in a corner. When she turned around to face Lazaro on his chair, he had his hungry cock in his hand: from shorts' split placket it reared like a blind white overfed eel from its grotto.

"Get over here."

Caozinha moved slowly across the room. Standing before Lazaro, arms at her sides, she kept her eyes on the floor.

"Take off your dress."

Caozinha pulled first one arm inside her sleeveless shift, then the other. But Lazaro grew impatient. He unhanded his cock, bent to grasp the garment's hem, and lifted the dress off over her head, before tossing it aside.

In the process, the fabric caught on one lumpy earring, stretching the flesh of Caozinha's lobe, causing her to wince but not to complain.

Naked, Caozinha appeared both more and less mature than when clothed. Her breasts were small but ripe-nippled, her hips narrow. Only a small amount of hair furzed her cunt mound, and a certain stolid pelvic thrust to her natural stance brought her cunt itself into unusual prominence, its upper notch like a potter's thumbprint against the chestnut glaze of her skin.

Lazaro flicked his cock to draw her eyes to it. "Wet it as I showed you."

Caozinha dribbled spit into first one hand, then the other. She reached down to Lazaro's dick and gripped it as if it were a truncheon. Her thumbs hooked, but only the first joints of her fingers overlapped. She worked her saliva up and down along the solid thickness, hooding and unhooding the head.

"Stop. Turn around."

Standing to the left of the seated giant, Caozinha presented her rump. Lazaro clamped her by the waist and, with strength to spare, lifted her entirely off her feet. Evidently practiced, she crooked her knees so that her dangling legs would not interfere with his intended lofting of her. A smile below his mustache like a gap in a hedge, he poised her over his slickened cock. Caozinha dropped her legs so that they trellised the path of his flesh, and he began to lower her. When the wide head of his penis first pushed inside her little slit, her feet were still two inches off the floorboards. Regaining contact with the floor, her legs to either side of his, she was firmly impaled. Lazaro continued to guide her descent until she sat against him.

"Now butter it. Butter that hot loaf in your oven."

Bracing her hands on Lazaro's furred legs near his knees, Caozinha commenced to fuck energetically, rising to toetip, then slamming back down. The brave chair complained but held as Lazaro met her movements with reciprocal heaves. His loose hairy dugs wobbled over a dense layer of pectoral muscle. He moved his hands up to her breasts to pinch and roll her nipples. He began hoarsely to whisper:

"Your mother was a slut too, was she not? An india cocksucker. But you are much worse. You would fuck a treeroot, if I did not keep your cunt so full. Ah, stop at the top a moment—there, now slide down—slowly! She wanted my name, your mother. She wanted you to have it too. But there is no way you are mine, dark girl. Your mother fucked too many men before she met her death. Your father was probably a sailor visiting Bahia from some distant land. Maybe an Arab from Africa. Do you think so? Did your mother fuck a camelfucker to make you? The way you carry burdens, maybe some of the camel blood got into yours."

Caozinha did not respond to Lazaro's assertions or questions, and so long as she continued to work his cock, he seemed not to care. As her frenzy mounted, he reached his right hand around to her clit, scooping up both her small breasts with the left. His blunt rotatory caress drew a squeal from her, and as if on a signal, Lazaro sluiced his jism up her in a brute bucking.

The stressed chair stridulated like an insect samba as the still-coupled pair relaxed backward. Lazaro poured himself another drink. Only after his erection had dwindled sufficiently was Caozinha able to dismount.

"Get dressed," ordered Lazaro, "and tidy up this place. Then collect a bushel of husks for the stove. I am going to sleep again. The writing came hard last night. And be quiet while you work inside."

Cum slimed her thighs. Caozinha pulled on her dress and used it to sop the spill from her vagina, splotching the dun fabric. She retrieved the broom from beneath the bed where Lazaro already reclined, and began to sweep. Soon, snores dueted with the broom's humble shushings.

In one poorly lit corner of the shack, Caozinha discovered a tumulus of crumpled pages. She looked back over her shoulder at Lazaro, who continued to assault the air with his snortings. Broom tucked under one arm, Caozinha bent to retrieve a sheet. Stepping into better illumination, she smoothed the pencil-tracked sheet to wrinkled flatness and read.

THE SHE BEAST
By Lazaro Sabino

No one in the little isolated jungle-shrouded village knew from whence the strange woman came. Like a rock heaved up from deep below the surface by the churning of the earth's guts, she

simply appeared one day, to the consternation of
all the narrow-minded citizens.

The first one to encounter her was a poor
housewife named Thais, who went to draw water
from the communal well—

The truncated story appeared not to interest Caozinha,
for she did not bother to investigate any more of the abortive text, instead disposing of the papers inside the
stove's cold ashy belly. Finished restoring the meager
contents of the hut to their best order, she took an empty
woven basket, smaller than her pannier, which sat
stoveside and let herself quietly out the dragging door.

An extravagant wash of chlorophyll-sieved sunlight
caused Caozinha to stop just outside the closed door of
the shack and blink for a few moments. Once her eyes
were accustomed to the jubilant rays, she set about her
task. Picking up the driest of the debris cast down by the
nut-eaters, she quickly accumulated a bushel's worth.
She placed the full basket by the door, and straightened
up with a more relaxed demeanor. Moving idly about the
clearing, she began to hum the same song she had earlier
drummed.

On the periphery of the clearing, where Bahia's typical
vegetative flood had met the ukase of the trees and halted,
Caozinha began to look with alertness for something.
Moving a ways into the thigh-brushing foliage until she
was out of sight of the hut, she eventually found her
prize: a sprawling, aloe-like succulent, a picket of soft
spears. She plucked a juicy stalk from the plant—its severed end drooled—and crushed it to a cool pulp. Drawing
up her hem, she applied the jelly tenderly to her cunt.

"Do you have any water?"

Caozinha jumped and gave a shrill cry.

A tall, full-figured woman—dressed in light clothing
suitable for the city, once fine but now somewhat ripped
and stained—stood only a few feet distant. Her white face
appeared kindly in a neutral way, but the partial domino
of a grapey birthmark lent her the air of being masked.

Caozinha did not answer immediately, and as if to explain her request further, the woman raised her hand.

Unmoving ants coated the lifted hand as if stuck to
honey, a patchy chitinous second skin.

"These make me thirsty," said the woman, and she tongued the insects off her skin in only four broad passes, palm first, knuckleside next.

Caozinha found speech. "Yes, there is water back at the shack."

"Good. Show me."

"But my master—"

"Master?"

"The man I live with. He does not appreciate visitors."

The woman snuffled delicately, her nostrils flaring. "Has he just fucked you?"

Caozinha hung her head. "Yes."

"Come here."

Caozinha obeyed. The woman reached beneath Caozinha's shift and swiped a finger's worth of unalloyed sperm from her leg. That tidbit of pearly mucus followed the ants. After a moment, the woman spoke:

"He is no problem. Come along."

Respectfully, an awed expression dominating her small face, Caozinha brought up the rear as the woman stepped gracefully through the vegetation. Once in the clearing, the stranger strode determinedly for the hut.

"What is your name?" Caozinha inquired timidly.

"She Beast."

Caozinha said nothing for a few steps. Then: "She Beast, the water lies this way." Caozinha pointed toward a crude collecting apparatus half-hidden by green shadows. A large square piece of sailcloth, four ropes clutching grommetted corners, was stretched like a low canopy or giant hammock between four trees. Beneath the drooping hole-punched center of the raincatcher stood a barrel to hoard the frequent stormwaters.

The woman changed course for the rainbutt, and Caozinha trailed her. At the barrel, after pushing up the sagging belly of the damp canopy the woman plunged her head directly in and drank, seemingly oblivious to the insects floating on the surface. After some time she raised her satisfied face, and water runnelled unheeded from her chin.

"Let us go see your master now."

Refraining from giving any advice, Caozinha accompanied the woman to the hut. The stranger did not knock or announce herself, but simply tugged the recalcitrant door open and stepped inside.

A MOUTHFUL OF TONGUES

As if sensing a spiky foreign newness within the cloistered space, Lazaro instantly awoke. Sitting up, bare feet thumping the floorboards, he appeared unsurprised, letting his eyes rove for a long minute over the white woman.

"Who are you?"

"She Beast."

Lazaro vented a gruff blast of disbelief. "My ass you are. You must have been talking to this traitorous little bitch. But who cares about names? What do you want here?"

"I want a place to live for a time. And some company."

Lazaro itched his jaw, overlong crusty nails rasping beard. "And what do you have to offer for my hospitality?"

"The fulfillment of dreams you will not even name."

"I have none such."

"Shall I show you just a little?"

"Go ahead."

The woman unfastened her skirt, dropped it and stepped from its folds. She peeled off her lavender shirt and stood naked save for sandals. In the kerosene light, she looked molten, legs twin columns of brass.

Caozinha stepped backward toward the door, but Lazaro halted her with a command. "Stay here and watch, you unfaithful slut. Be our duenna. You might learn something."

Slump-shouldered, Caozinha sat herself down in a chair. Watchful yet reserved, she fingered her cheap earrings meditatively as the woman advanced on Lazaro.

"Let me take these off," said the woman. She tucked agile fingers beneath the waistband of Lazaro's shorts and drew them down. His brawny pale ass and thighs were as hairy as the generally exposed, slightly darker portion of his legs. Despite its recent explosive gouting, his big cock stood attentive again, massive balls sacked below.

"Would you like to fuck my tits?" The woman pushed her breasts together. "The little one cannot offer that."

Lazaro leered, and dropped his hands on her shoulders. "Get on your knees then."

The woman kneeled and arched backwards slightly from her waist, stomach hummocking. Lazaro bestrode her, his own knees angled to a small degree, in order to valley his cock between her breasts. Two-handedly, she squashed her tits together to enfold his cock.

Then she released her breasts. Miraculously, they adhered along the length of his cock as if glued tight.

"A good trick—" began Lazaro, then stopped, plainly amazed.

Outwardly, her juxtaposed breasts revealed nothing but a slight oscillation of their satiny surfaces, like faint ripples on a pond from a school of minnows swimming not far below. But within the new passage formed by their interface, more aggressive extractive and caressive motions must have been occurring.

Lazaro began to squirm, but seemed unable or unwilling either to withdraw or to thrust. The woman dropped one hand into her own crotch and used the other to cup a cheek of Lazaro's ass. Her nipples described small nutations reflective of the luxurious turmoil inside the factitious flesh tube.

After some minutes, Lazaro, red-faced, seemed ready to cum, but the woman counseled sternly, "Not yet you cannot," and continued to work her clit. The signal of her readiness for their mutual orgasm was the gaping of her mouth to allow her tongue to drape her chin: more extensively than normal in most anyone else, but not without human precedence.

From the open top of the woman's mammary tube burst forth jets of cum to dot the carpet of her tongue, which humped upward in the middle to land the first, most energetic globules bound otherwise for cheek or nose. Later lazy drops landed below her chin, but were swabbed up by the tips of her questing tongue.

Lazaro sagged in his awkward stance, the woman's breasts fell unaided apart into their normal configuration (formerly hidden epidermis undistinguished in any way), and she slithered easily out from below him and onto her feet. Lazaro dropped back exhaustedly onto the bed.

"You can stay," he rasped. "Caozinha, get her some food."

Caozinha's face retained its stolid blankness, but her breathing mimicked a runner's. She stood up, but the woman halted her.

"That will not be necessary. I am already full."

A MOUTHFUL OF TONGUES

* * *

A calendrical montage of arcing suns and moons flashing across the dome of day or night, of clouds and rain and storm's bright cessation, of drudgery and carnality, of slow quiet stretches of innocent activities alternating with explosive bouts of rampageous fucking, a tornado of limbs and a monsoon of squirting fluids.

Caozinha's routine over the days immediately following the advent of the She Beast changed little. To the mestiza fell the maintenance of the household, the sweepings, gatherings, cookings, washings and repairings, enough work to keep her busy for at least half of each day. (Her free time she spent mostly outside, never straying far from the clearing and casting frequent looks around as if for the anonymous child-sized follower that had shadowed her last trip from the town.) The only chore stripped from Caozinha was sex with Lazaro. That task the She Beast undertook with all enthusiasm.

Sharing Lazaro's creakingly guyed mattress at night, the She Beast permuted her alien flesh for the giant's manifold gargantuan desires. Above or below or beside the man, she circumscribed his tenderest parts in novel ways unheard of by mere mortals. They climaxed howlingly several times each night, and often a time or two by daylight. And most of these metamorphic couplings Caozinha witnessed from her shallow pallet on the floor, the narrow confines of the hut permitting no secrecy or privacy, her master allowing no escape, even if some refuge elsewhere, nonexistent, had been beckoning.

Yet Caozinha, though non-participant, never averted her gaze.

During the times between the saturating sex, Caozinha spoke only when addressed. Save once:

Only the two women occupied the hut, Lazaro away using their rude outhouse. Caozinha turned from her current labors—sewing a patch on a pair of Lazaro's shorts—and said, "Do you not ever feel the need to get outside for some fresh air?"

Shipwrecked on the shoals of the bed, the She Beast replied, "Why? I have everything I need right within these four walls."

When Lazaro was not fucking, sleeping, or devouring their comestibles so heedlessly that Caozinha's next shopping trip would surely arrive sooner than expected, he kept busy writing. The arrival of the She Beast, a creature ostensibly straight from his own imagination, seemed to have opened a conduit previously blocked. Seated at the teetering table, he applied pencil to paper with feverish industry, accumulating more pages deemed worthy for preserving in a neat stack than those fit for stove-tinder.

One morning Lazaro took down from a high dark-cornered shelf a spavined typewriter big and unwieldy as a donkey engine. He placed it on the table, which tottered like a newborn foal until braced against a wall. He selected and arranged a dozen sheets of manuscript beside the machine. He inserted fresh paper beneath platen. He sat and began to peck away with two blunt fingers.

Caozinha stared at the spectacle. The She Beast lay abed for a time, eyes closed but patently not asleep. Unclothed, her opalescent body exhibited a magnetic appeal, a chalk goddess turfed out of some neolithic hillside. But Lazaro ignored both the woman and the girl. Eventually, the two spectators went outside, Caozinha first, the She Beast following half an hour later, still aggressively nude.

They met by the rainbutt. The She Beast initiated a short conversation.

"How often does he do this?"

"Not at all in the last year."

"I tried to suck his cock, but he pushed me away."

"That does not surprise me."

The She Beast seemed sunk in thought. "Maybe Lazaro and I can fuck when he is finished."

Caozinha turned away. "More than likely."

The staccato mechanical clatter issuing from the shack kept Caozinha and the She Beast at bay until early afternoon. Upon the clatter's termination, the two women both drifted deliberately back.

Inside the patchwork hut, Lazaro was stuffing with some care the fair copy of his stories into a canvas shoulder bag.

"Caozinha! How much money do we have?"

"Ten claws, six scales, eighteen quills."

A MOUTHFUL OF TONGUES

"Get it for me!"

Caozinha retrieved the colorful bills and chunky silver coins from the ex-flour canister where they were kept and laid them on the table next to the shoulder bag.

Lazaro tugged his shorts down. His bare-assed massiveness seemed to occlude half the cabin. "Are my town clothes clean? I have to see Tinoco at the newspaper, and I don't want him making stupid comments about my looks again."

Caozinha moved to the clumsily assembled cedar storage chest from which she had recently taken the shorts for patching, and began to assemble Lazaro's traveling outfit.

Aquamarine eyes afire, the She Beast sidled up to the naked Lazaro and grabbed his dangling cock, thick even when flaccid. "Can we do it now, Lazaro?"

As his answer, Lazaro took her by the waist and rotated her to face away from him. "Bend over."

The She Beast spread her feet apart, leaned forward and cupped her own knees, Lazaro's hands still riding her upper hips. Her cunt, glistening imbricate carnelian labia spelling an irresistible invitation, hove into sharp display. Stiffening instantly, Lazaro guided himself deeply into her. The She Beast groaned, and Lazaro replied, "Up into your belly, girl."

Without forewarning, the She Beast lifted her left leg up and backward, to crook around behind Lazaro. Her right leg followed suit, and now, her ankles locked, her arms extended like a diver's, she wheelbarrowed the man who continued to hold her midsection. Solid breasts swaying minimally, she began to work his prick with the unique inner strangulatory components of her symbiotic cunt.

Midway through the fuck came a startling reversal: in a half-perceptible compressed sequence of movements, the She Beast unlocked her ankles and spun herself in the cradle of Lazaro's hands to face the ceiling, her legs swapping sides in a complicated tuck-and- fold aerial ballet, her cunt never relinquishing its hold. Her aubergine facial birthmark leaped into view, as if suddenly formed by splatters of colored rain from a leak above. A snarl of a smile cleaved her face.

Startled, Lazaro released his hold on her.

Miraculously, the She Beast did not slump or sag. Stomach like a cask, her spine and pelvis some machined armature, muscles cabling in her newly rewrapped legs, she continued to cantilever from her partner at a right angle, fixed as a limb from a tree, and the merciless working of her cunt skipped not a beat. She moved her hands to palm her own ass.

Recovered, Lazaro began vigorously to palpate her tits. Both attained their orgasmic culmination within minutes of the switch.

Sated for the moment, the She Beast disengaged and moved to the bed. Lazaro's cock, filigreed with a translucent vaginal gel, deflated as fast as it had risen.

"My clothes, Caozinha!"

"Here they are."

Dressing, Lazaro explained: "Unless I am a bigger fool than I ever believed, Tinoco is going to buy all three of these stories, and we will make some serious money for the first time in a long while. Not to mention bolstering both my reputation and that of the *Messenger of the North*, that rag! But I might have to wine and dine the bastard first, so do not expect me back here until tomorrow."

Caozinha said, "Very well."

But the She Beast said nothing.

As Lazaro disappeared down the path—straw hat at a jaunty angle, blue shirt and white pants like some simplistic flag, shoulder bag swaying with the energy of his stride—Caozinha watched with an unreadable expression on her halfbreed features.

As if riding an express train, the sun steamed below the green crowns of the treetops, and soon thereafter beneath the horizon. Velvet-wrapped night brought the usual arboreal symphony, featuring insect chorus and the mortal call-and-response of nocturnal predators and prey.

With the lantern extinguished, the interior of the windowless shack was a blind cave. Previously, at dusk, Caozinha had hefted her drooping pallet and hesitated at the door, as if contemplating spending a night outside, before returning to her accustomed spot. The She Beast had not left the bed since Lazaro's departure.

In the middle of the night, moonlight asymmetrically rimming the slumping door, the She Beast spoke.

"Caozinha."

Caozinha's reply came instantly. "Why do you use my name for the first time, She Beast?"

"Caozinha, I am lonely."

"You stole my master from me, and now you wish me to be your friend."

"We do not have to be friends. We can just fuck."

"No."

"All right. Come sleep with me then. I promise I will not touch you all night."

"Promise? By what token?"

"By my cunt."

Caozinha said nothing for a time. Then came a rustling, three slapping footfalls, and the creaking of the webbed bed frame.

"You came. Thank you."

"You gave the only bond I could believe you would honor."

Hours passed. A singular set of slow breaths affirmed an individual sleep.

The irregular band of moonlight around the door began to widen. Wood ground softly against earth. When opened to its fullest extent, the door framed a child-sized mannikin in silhouette, hesitant with one hand clutching the door, one outstretched as if to cling to another not yet offered.

"Go away," whispered the She Beast, not unkindly. "We will meet later."

The frozen figure pivoted slowly, as if reluctant to obey, but then departed.

Sunlight flooded the hut along the privileged channel offered by the open door, highlighting the grain of the floorplanks, segments of the legs of table and bed.

Lying on her back, Caozinha opened her eyes. The She Beast kneeled alongside the mestiza's head.

"Now it is the morning."

The kneeling woman swung a leg over the recumbent girl's head.

"Can you feel the heat of my cunt? Can you smell how it wants you?"

Straddled but yet unpinned, Caozinha could have slipped away. But she didn't move.

The She Beast lowered her twat toward the mestiza's face.

When pendulous twat met mouth, the She Beast's cunt initiated a convoluted kiss. Inner labia actively insinuated themselves beneath Caozinha's lips, inching along her gums in delicate massage, while the major labia played and nipped outside, like a tapir's finessing buccal appendage.

Then something very like Caozinha's own tongue delved out of the cunt and into the mestiza's mouth.

The She Beast maintained this slow-writhing kiss for nearly a quarter of an hour. Both of Caozinha's hands had crawled to her own cunt to pleasure herself.

Each woman came in tectonic shivers. The She Beast removed her cunt from Caozinha's face, leaving behind a glycerine swath. Caozinha's eyes had rolled partly backward, exposing mostly whites, but the slow-fading activity of her hands in her lap indicated awareness.

"Now I will give you something you can really enjoy."

The She Beast brought her face down to Caozinha's humid cunt, and opened her mouth to fullest dilation.

The swollen head of a large handsome prick, drops of clear lubricant oozing from its vertical eye, emerged from the She Beast's mouth. The pulsing cock bridged the inches between mouth and cunt and poked into Caozinha, who released a gasp. With ridged head gaining such a firm purchase, the rest of the autonomous shaft quickly transferred to its new abode. Last to emerge from the She Beast's mouth, flopping out over the pale of her teeth, were the requisite testicles, walled behind with a drumhead of flesh. Flush against Caozinha's perineum, the balls joggled in accord with the hidden accordioning of their attached cock.

The She Beast stood up and turned around at a sound.

Lazaro filled the doorway, rumpled and hung-overish, shirt wine-stained and pants misbuttoned.

"You lousy bitches!"

He stomped to the bed and lifted Caozinha by her nightclothes.

"Get out of my goddamn bed!" He threw her across the shack to her pallet, where she crumpled, the autonomous cock still obliviously active inside her, cycling through elaborate compression and expansion.

The She Beast sought to paste herself against Lazaro. "She pleaded with me, Lazaro. She begged me for it."

A MOUTHFUL OF TONGUES

"Shut up, you whore!" Lazaro backhanded the woman across the face, massive hand cracking unmarked cheek to draw a color nearly matching her birthblot.

The transformation from seductress to avenger happened instantaneously. The short crop of dark hair on the She Beast's head erected like an angry cat's. Her face hived out in a rash of wrath. She swept her leg powerfully behind Lazaro's at the same time as she pushed him, and he toppled to the floor. Then she was atop him before he could react.

She raised her hands: from beneath longish nails that never lost their immaculate jade paint dripped pearls of liquid.

The She Beast plunged all ten nails into Lazaro's neck.

Sudden and complete catatonia whelmed the struggling giant.

Fast as her anger had risen, it disappeared. Now the She Beast smiled, and began to hum a wavering work-melody, all diligence and daVinci attention.

From the pores of her palms, a new cloudy liquid began to sweat.

The She Beast commenced a slow massage, beginning with Lazaro's face.

At first, wherever she touched, coarse close hair literally melted away, transformed to a trickle of waste fluid that dampened the floor. The She Beast passed her hands over Lazaro's entire ventral side, scything hair as a reaper cuts grain, until he was totally smooth. Effortlessly, she rolled him over, attended to his back, and then flipped him again.

Now the quality of her exudate changed, from superficial to penetrative, and she began to mold his flesh without shattering the container of his skin.

Like a master potter, she redistributed the compliant clay of his fatty gut. Part of it moved upward to bulk out his already sizable breasts into pleasant female amplitude. The rest went down to add curve to his hips. Both reassignments additionally contributed to a flat belly and shapely waist. She tinkered with his face, played in the region of his vocal cords, removed muscle bulk from his arms and legs (Lazaro's body lost hot liquid profusely, staining the floorboards), rolled out lusher nipples like a chef fashioning pasta, then paused briefly to admire her work.

Now the She Beast began the most challenging task.

Levering apart Lazaro's legs, she placed both hands against his big genitals and pushed them back into his pelvic basin. Keeping them there with one hand, she used the other to collect juice from her cunt. This gushing from her gash she applied to the trapped male genitals, and began to mold them. Her teasing, plucking and tweaking was met by a helpful autocatalytic response from the self-adapting genitals, now plainly vectoring toward the female.

Within moments, the transfiguration attained perfection.

Stretched out on the shack's floor was an alluring Amazon, sleek, full-breasted and possessed of a richly flowered cunt.

The She Beast moved to Caozinha's side. Throughout Lazaro's remodeling, the mestiza, oblivious even to being picked up and hurled away, had been swimming in a stream of orgasms from the dildoing of the living cock inside her.

The She Beast gripped the balls of Caozinha's implant, and the mestiza's ecstatic convulsions abruptly stopped. Sliding two fingers into Caozinha's cunt alongside the cock, the She Beast stretched the ligamental hole wide enough to stuff the cooperative balls inside.

Caozinha's mons now exhibited traveling bulges as interior movements propagated themselves in the form of mole-like swarmings.

From the mestiza's cunt emerged the sticky head of the self-reversed cock. The penis dropped fully out, followed by the balls.

But a firm deep root, freshly grown, anchored the equipment in the normal fashion, stopping complete detachment. The tackle joined flawlessly with the surrounding skin, damming forever Caozinha's converted cunt, now thoroughly ennervated into the prick.

The She Beast stopped to give Caozinha a conventional kiss, sharing a few potent drops of benthic saliva, then bestowed a similar buss on Lazaro.

Out the door, across the clearing, twixt slapping fronds: the forest swallowed her as easily and swiftly as soil claims the rain.

A MOUTHFUL OF TONGUES

Lazaro's eyes sprang open. Caozinha already kneeled beside the massive woman, stroking the recumbent figure's cheek and weeping.

"Mother," sobbed the young man.

A curious peace descended on the Amazon's features. "Son," she dulcetly replied.

* * *

Behind the main bar at The Blue Afternoon Hotel, a curving prow of dark polished sculpted wood, Arlindo Quincas briskly skippered his responsive yet inanimate crew of glasses and bottles. Squat pebbled tumblers, steep-sided shot thimbles, long-stemmed flutes, wide-mouthed crystal, big-handled octagonal mugs. Squarish, elongate or wasp-waisted liters, round-bellied flagons, flattish flasks, even one bottle shaped like a woman with arms upraised overhead to accept a cork between swandiver-braced hands. Temporarily resident in these motley bottles on their several journeys to assorted stomachs, the step-ranked liquors of a hundred colors doubled themselves in a long mirror.

In the subdued lighting—globed gas flames that hissed subliminally like angry djinns—necessary in the inner room even during the middle of the day, Quincas filled orders with stolid efficiency, splitting coconuts for fresh milk, squeezing limes, crushing ice. He loaded and reloaded the cork-lined tray of the quiet Dartpipe servant girl at frequent intervals. (Her restrained yet sensual stride evoked her signature quiet sourceless clicking, as if from metal heeltaps, yet oddly different.) From its shrinelike corner a new cabinet radio softly disbursed sambas, every note of which was swaddled in the fruity resonance of the receiver's cloth and wood frame.

Into the bar strolled one of the quintet who perpetually tenanted the hotel's veranda, the fattest idler. Laughing, he told Quincas, "This heat drives the drinks through me like rice through a housewife's mill! No mistake, I have to piss yet again! And I won't use your bushes like some I could name!"

The fat man disappeared into the water closet, and came out shortly thereafter.

"Did your bartender fail to appear again today?"

Quincas nodded solemnly, lips tight beneath his mustache. "I hate to fire anyone, especially someone who is experiencing the problems Galeno is enduring with that wife of his. Still, I might have to do so."

The burly patron scooped a handful of roasted seeds red as river mud and the size of buttons from the bowl on the bar, and flung them into his mouth like a handful of gravel thrown at a rat. Around his chewing, he said, "Be ruthless! That is my advice. How do you think I brought my business to such a pitch of smooth efficiency that I can afford to loll about your premises all day?"

Quincas sighed. "Running a hotel is vastly different from running a printshop, Ivo."

"Nonsense! It all boils down to a firm hand!"

Quincas interrupted his unasked-for business lesson to accept a drink order from the demure native waitress. He swiftly concocted the requisite cocktails and turned back to the sweating Ivo, who continued on a new tack:

"The five of us are planning a trip to the house of Senhora Graca, for this very Friday night. Will you come with us, Arlindo? Ricardo, Belmiro, Januario and Estevao—they all insisted I ask you. We think it would do you good. Graca promises some new girls by the end of the week, assuming the steamer from Three Lakes arrives on time."

"I will consider it."

"Do more than that! We fear your balls will burst! How long can you wait for your strange mistress to return? Face it, man—she never will!"

Quincas offered no rejoinder, but simply turned to crouch and shuffle in a cupboard as if for some urgently needed implement, and Ivo, unanswered, shrugged and left.

Half an hour passed. In the heat of mixing, Quincas blindly sought a glass from an empty rack, found nothing, cursed mildly, and stepped away from the bar and through a door. In a few moments he returned with a tray of clean moisture-beaded glasses.

Waiting at the bar was a newcomer who caused Quincas to start and nearly drop his burden.

Beneath his expensive natural-hued linen suit, the smallish yet bulky man seemed as solid as a keg of nails. Under a trig borsalino, his head resembled a small boulder positioned directly on his shoulders. Across his lithic face half a dozen knife scars glyphed a conqueror's triumphs as on some ancient stele.

Glassware chimed nervously as Quincas stepped to the bar to set his tray down. "Senhor Reymoa, what an honor. Please accept a drink with my sincere hospitality. What will you have?"

Reymoa settled one elegantly shod foot upon the brass bar-rail. He inspected Quincas intently before commanding, quietly yet forcefully, "Remove your shirt."

Not prone to quibble with this man, Quincas quickly did as instructed. When he stood bare from the waist up, the hotel owner was gratified to note that all the other patrons in the room were very conspicuously looking away, intent on not prying into Reymoa's business, however eccentrically intriguing.

"So, it is as they say." Reymoa reached out one hand—its two smallest fingers irregularly truncated, old scarring dense—and gripped Quincas's restored bicep. "Where is she? Where is the witch who gave you a new arm?"

"I have no idea, Senhor—" Reymoa squeezed, and Quincas winced. "I swear, this is the truth. Would I let such a prize slip from me, if I could have stopped her from leaving? She fled without telling me anything of her plans."

The imprint of Reymoa's grip faded slowly, blood resuffusing the white outline of fingers and palm. "You will certainly tell me if she returns."

"Of course, of course, how could I not share—"

"Meanwhile, I will search for her with my own men. Do you have a tintype of her perhaps?"

"No, nothing of the sort."

"Describe her then."

Quincas painted a word-picture of the woman he knew as Senhorita Yemana. His glowing description threatened to become fulsome, until Reymoa cut him short.

"Enough. I have other important business to attend to now."

Quincas addressed the departing man's back. "This has been my pleasure, Senhor Reymoa."

At the exit to the bar, Reymoa halted without warning and turned back to Quincas.

"My daughter makes her debut into society this Friday evening, upon her fifteenth birthday. You will receive an invitation."

"An honor, an honor, Senhor, to celebrate the coming out of young Senhorita Darciana."

"That is as it should be."

Reymoa had been gone for thirty seconds before Quincas recaptured enough presence of mind to redon his shirt, and an additional fifteen minutes passed before his jitters eased completely. During that time, the calls for drinks ebbed, until finally the mid-afternoon lull was well underway, the horse latitudes of inebriation.

Quincas summoned the waitress with the shake of a handbell. She arrived as always (click-click, click-click), exhibiting simple jungle graces and downcast gaze.

"Do the quintet of gossips have a full pitcher?"

"Yes, Senhor."

"Come with me then."

Quincas conducted his employee through corridors closed to patrons until they reached a locked door. With a key from a well-stocked ring, Quincas let them inside.

Sacks of flour and sugar elevated on splintery pallets formed knee-high burlap couches separated by narrow aisles. Shelves of canned goods and bottled preserves lined the walls of the room. A not-unpleasant odor from old sweet and sour spills, lingering despite scrupulous cleaning, permeated the room. The sun peered in through an iron-framed skylight.

"Take off your clothes, Yeena."

The woman undressed easily, without resistance, blouse and skirt swiftly draped across a stack. She retained coarse cotton hose gartered above the knee, as well as her high-topped leather shoes.

Nude, the india instantly showed one of the peculiarities of her tribe: hypnotic whorls of black tattooing mapped her conical breasts.

Quincas began to unbutton his pants. "Lie down."

Yeena sat first on the edge of a floursack pile, then reclined backward, a sienna odalisque. She drew her feet up off the floor and dug the heels of her shoes into the burlap's seams for purchase. Then she spread her legs.

Two blue stone rings—lapis shaved flat as a coin—pierced her minor labia, one to a side. A narrow slit visible in the circumference of the left ring revealed how they had first entered her flesh. The weight of this rare coinage drew her lips into a perpetual invitation. As she boosted her ass into a more comfortable position, the rings knocked and stonily chirped.

Quincas climbed between the india's legs. Only semi-erect, he seemed to be having difficulty becoming fully aroused, a hurdle he sought to leap by applying himself to Yeena's breasts, tonguing her nipples and mouthing each runic tit in turn to well beyond its palmoil-orange areola. After some time, he delivered his unwieldy prick into her cunt and began to stroke.

Wearing a face of accustomed acceptance, Yeena reached down and inserted a forefinger into each ring, using them to pull her cunt lips apart. But despite this enticement and her general cooperation—she whispered over and over an enigmatic native word, "tulikawa," as inducement—Quincas huffed away only to a gradual but undeniable atrophy of his cock, without experiencing any satisfaction. Sighing, he removed himself from the woman.

"Get dressed and go back to work."

"Yes, Senhor."

After Yeena had gone (annular stones kissing discreetly yet noisily), Quincas sat disconsolately on the rough sack, contemplating his traitorous prick. Finally rising to get dressed and resume his own tiresome duties, he murmured, "My bruja, my witch . . . Where are you? Please return!"

* * *

From the vantage of a screeching gull or skua aloft, the Blue Afternoon Hotel could be seen to sit at the edge of a well-defined district (low shabby buildings jammed together like weary harvesters sleeping in an airless shed; narrow cobbled streets; no vegetation save the monkey-puzzle trees that ringed and demarcated the neighborhood) whose outline roughly evoked the semblance of a cat's head seen sidelong: ears, muzzle, neck, and the lone eye a communal low-coped well surrounded by a small cobbled plaza. To the east of this feline portion of the town, beyond an intervening park and beach, the sea reigned, a choppy viridian coverlet spread over marine mysteries, the old harbor fort regnant like a weary yet un-

77

dismayed Canute. To the north rose a hilly, almost mountainous neighborhood, its terraced land stabbed with big houses on sprawling estates. A small funicular railway sent its gaudy toylike cars up and down the steepest slope in a perpetual parade. Dominating the west were numerous small factories; the southern precincts boasted all the best shops, as well as state offices and the warrens of lawyers.

As dusk fell, scattered lights—mallowtorch, gas, and the rare incandescent—prinked on in the neighborhood shaped like the cat's head. The streets filled with people whose faces exhibited an ancient complementarity: buyers and sellers, revelers and promoters, users and the used, givers and takers. Musicians poured lively notes from flutes, guitars and bandeons into the streets like sonic recapitulations of the early-morning sidewalk hosings undertaken by café owners. The enticing aromas of coffee, broiling fish, barbecued pork, prawn stew, and fermented cactus drink dispensed from purple-glass basketed demijohns fought with their nightly antagonists: the stenches of piss, horse manure, slops, and unclean flesh. Mediating between the olfactory camps, sandalwood incense diplomatically insinuated its coils. Occasionally, a vagrant sea breeze would wander lazily through, momentarily overwhelming the native scents.

In the Snout, a bar named Tooth and Whiskers inhaled and exhaled patrons like a mighty lung: men paired with their women, interlocked hands swinging with exaggerated vivaciousness or arms wrapped around waists; stag packs of either sex, giggling or hooting; hustlers male, female or interdenominational; hawkers of newspapers, shaved ice rainbowed with syrups, cigarettes and lottery tickets; the odd policeman, wearing an eager demeanor slanted more toward a free meal than an arrest.

The customers leaving the Tooth and Whiskers naturally showed the effects of their stay. Stumbling or capering, slurring or shouting their words, exchanging sloppy punches or equally sloppy kisses, they exited like seeds scattered from an exploding fruit, each to his own square of soil deemed home.

Long after midnight, a man and woman teetered out of the bar. Hanging drunkenly onto each other, they tripped off down the street. The man showed the bulk of a stevedore or sailor, and wore garments befitting either trade:

tight blue-striped shirt, loose woolen trousers, plaited huaraches. The woman's flouncy black blouse fell off her shoulders; her crimson skirt pied with images of frangipani and heliotrope flowers threatened to snag its hem on her spike-heeled shoes with each giddy step.

The pair teetered down the mostly empty street, woman giggling, man groping, their destination seemingly eluding them like a marble in a tilted maze, as gauged by their veering several times in directions contrary to their previous course.

At last, elusive haven no closer, the man pulled the woman into an alley, a channel of deeper darkness, puddled and putrid. Halting only a foot or two inside, the man braced the woman against one brick wall. A wand of streetlight vertexed the man and woman at waist-level, rendering them bifurcate creatures.

"I mean to fuck you right here, Lenira." He bunched her skirt up around her waist, revealing her bareness below.

"Oh, Gozo, no—wait until we can reach my bed."

"My prick won't let me. Feel it in my pants, Lenira."

"It *is* huge, Gozo. Oh, yes, I *will* let you. Your touch on my cunt is so gentle, like —"

"Your cunt? But both my hands are still freeing my hungry cock for you, Lenira—"

The woman looked down.

What seemed a mere mound of dirty rags had crept or otherwise materialized beneath her. An extension of the trashpile very much resembling a swaddled arm had lifted up from the mass and was stroking her vagina.

Lenira screamed, and Gozo swore. He stepped back and launched a forceful kick at the ragheap. Contrary to expectations, the rags did not fly apart, but merely trapped his foot. Lenira leaped aside in instinctive fright, skirt swirling, and Gozo bent to free his foot, punching at the rags.

The rags silently exploded, wrapping themselves around Gozo's head. Gozo staggered upright, clawing at the cloth concealing his features. From beneath the crazy living turban, his muffled cries for help lasted only a few seconds, before they too ceased and he collapsed upon his back to the stones.

Lenira made an abortive move toward her fallen lover, then plainly thought better of it. Slowly, she backed up toward the alley mouth. Attaining the street, she broke into a nearly ankle-twisting run.

The unbreathing corpse of Gozo lay for a few moments undisturbed, still wearing its unfashionably suffocating scarf. Then from the street came the padding of bare feet.

The entry to the alley was blocked by the silhouette of a good-sized woman. She wore man's garb, some orders too big: shirt ballooning around her, waist of her trousers bunched with a length of tar-tipped rope. She turned her head to look up and down the street: an empurpled terra incognita across one irregular hemisphere of her face testified to the shabby ignorance of all spiritual cartographers.

Kerry Hackett, Senhorita Yemana, She Beast: the woman moved swiftly into the alley and bent over the corpse.

"Get off him, Bloodchild."

The creature formed of ennervated, menstrually and salivarily seeded cotton scraps recohered from two-dimensionality into its toddler form. The woman extended her arms and the ragthing jumped up into her embrace. Coiled arms lovingly noosed her neck.

"My poor baby. I know you were never born properly. That is all my fault. And now you suffer. Well, let us see what we can do for you."

The Bloodchild snuggled into her bosom more closely. The woman crooned to it for a time, then gently set it down.

"But first, we cannot let the essence of this one go to waste."

She dropped effortlessly to her knees beside Gozo's body. His cock, haired halfway up its length, lay partially outside his unfastened pants, and she levered it completely out.

Under her manual secretory ministrations, a subset of fading cells rekindled and responded. Gozo's dick stiffened, the woman's green nails studding his prick like beetles on a cornstalk. After only a few strokes, he jetted upward forcefully one final time.

The woman's lashing bactrian tongue caught the sperm straight from the air. A single good-sized drop splashed the dank pavement, but she found that one too.

Bloodchild trotting to keep up with its mother, the pair departed the alleyway.

A MOUTHFUL OF TONGUES

The flow of revelers in the streets of the Catshead district had diminished dramatically. Keeping to chocolaty shadows and deep doorways, the woman and the ragthing remained unnoticed or ignored. After an hour or so, the pair could be found threading their way down a path through the band of drowsing trees separating the grim neighborhood from The Blue Afternoon. A shuffling of tired feet on the path sounded from the direction of the hotel, and both woman and creature melted into the foliage.

Down the path moved a lone man, thin and pensive in the available starlight. Stooped from both the day's work and a perceptible psychic burden, the man mumbled to himself.

"Gercina, why must you put me through this torture? For what, for what? After so many years of failure, why must you persist in your obsessions? Your folly is destroying us!"

The man moved on reluctantly toward some uncomfortable destination, his despairing monologue drifting into unintelligibility. Behind him at a small distance followed the woman and her charge.

A small multifamily dwelling near the Eye: trampled dirt yard, scattered trash unattractive even to scavengers, tattered clothes left overnight on a line. The man let himself into the first floor apartment, where light spilled forth from a rear window. The pair of followers moved to a hidden vantage beneath the windowsill and into spying position. Nocturnal insects thrummed and trilled a discordant concerto.

A paraffin lamp illuminated scuffed wallpaper patterned with songbirds. A bureau held a shrine: lit votive candle, icons of saints and pagan godlings, an advertisement torn from a magazine depicting children at play. On a neatly made bed lay a naked woman: black as alluvial soil, she possessed a face placid as an ox's, breasts like pudding and hips broad as a delta. Her right hand rested in her tangled bush, languidly massaging her clit.

The inner door opened, and the man from the path entered. Stubbled face like a sad horse's, he wore a black silk vest over a white shirt, bow-tie and dark trousers.

"Galeno, I have been waiting so long for you," said the woman.

"I know, I know, Gercina. Just give me a moment, please. The bar held more customers than you have ever seen, and Senhor Quincas was exceedingly demanding tonight. Despite that miraculous arm of his, I sense that all is not well with him."

Gercina paid no heed to Galeno's tribulations. "You have to fuck me now, Galeno. It is a husband's duty."

Loosening his tie and collar, Galeno said, "But we did it this morning and also before I left for work at one. Can you still be in need?"

"You know that is not the issue. We have to make a child. I want a child, Galeno."

Galeno had stripped to his underwear, sleeveless ribbed shirt and worn boxers, revealing long skinny limbs like celery stalks. "But all the years of trying have brought us no success. Should we not reconsider our mutual lives in this light?"

"But my sister—"

"Jesus, woman, enough with your damn sister!"

Gercina began copiously to weep. Galeno sat on the bed beside her, boxsprings giving iron voice. "Now, now, I spoke without thinking, dear. Please forgive me—"

Within minutes, Galeno was swamped within Gercina's embrace as a lone soldier might have been surrounded by a whole division. On her back still, the plush Negro woman pincered her pallid partner with her sturdy legs and fumbled his cock out of his shorts. Her primed cunt wetly swallowed his twice-milked dick and she bounced her weary partner to a third climax.

Exhausted, Galeno pulled out, rolled over to his side of the bed, and fell deeply asleep within seconds.

Gercina closed her eyes, a satisfied smile wreathing her face. She herself appeared near the shores of sleep but not yet embarked.

The white woman lurking outside sprang silently into the room, clearing the windowframe without touching it, landing feather-light. Behind her, the ragthing pulled itself laboriously up and inside, the noise of its struggles no louder than a load of laundry tumbling out of its hamper and down a flight of stairs. The barefoot female intruder padded over to the sleeping form of the husband. (Gercina's eyes also remained shut.) She raised her hand, two fingers extending in papal blessing, nails exuding droplets. She drew her benedictory fingers across the man's lips, and he seemed to drop deeper into unconsciousness.

Now the woman kneeled on the bed, causing Gercina's eyes to shoot open in alarm.

"Who are you! Get out of here! Galeno! Galeno!"

Kerry pulled her shirt over her head, spilling her tits out, and tugged the tar-splotched slipknot holding up her pants: her cunt flashed pink as she discarded her trousers. "Be quiet. Your husband will not awaken until I allow it."

Gercina's eyes widened. "You are a woman. What do you want? We have no money—"

The white woman returned no answer. Instead she simply gripped Gercina's ankles and effortlessly lifted the black woman's legs up and toward the ceiling to bring the negress's cunt into view: a dark iris flower dewed with pearly snailings.

"Will this do, Bloodchild? Do you like this one?"

The cotton toddler appeared at the side of the bed and wordlessly signalled its assent.

"My sweet Lord! What is that—"

"Your baby."

Gercina began a scream promptly cut off by Kerry's squirting palm laid across her mouth. This nonviolent stifling seemed also to remove Gercina's will to struggle, although she remained visibly conscious. Kerry dropped the black woman's heavy legs back onto the mattress, then, moving to knee them wider, positioned herself between them.

"First we must remove the dead seed of your husband and prepare your womb for my son."

Kerry reached down between her own legs. Jade-tipped fingers slipped between her articulated cunt lips and teased out the spatulate head of a sizable prick. Slowly but steadily coaxing out her masculine member, she soon showed nearly twelve inches of prominently veined cock anchored somewhere deep within her cunt.

Kerry hooked Gercina's legs behind the knees with her elbows. The head of the dangling alien cock chanced to touch Gercina's inner thigh and seemed to stick by its tiny mouth. Kerry used one hand to grasp her cock and pull it away from Gercina's thigh. The black woman's flesh tented outward, as if held to the prickhead by a vacuum, but a moderate tug eventually released her skin.

Bringing the suctioning cock to Gercina's well-greased cunt, Kerry inserted several inches of it. Then she was pulled closer, mons to mons, more as if reeled in by the slithering cock than through any pushing forward of her hips. Kerry bent down and applied her lips to Gercina's. The black woman's gaze assumed even more startled proportions. White breasts flattened black, nipple sliding off nipple like moist berries in a bowl.

No outward pumping could be seen, but Gercina's ass jiggled seismically, as if some kind of uterine furrowing were transpiring.

Kerry finished decisively upon some moment whose perfection was known only to her. She pulled away from Gercina, no cock now in evidence anywhere. She extended a hand to the ragbaby, who had been earnestly watching the preparations for its human embodiment, and the creature matched her grip to be pulled up onto the bed.

A maternal hand on either side of the creature's bandagelike head, Kerry whispered, "Goodbye, my little one. May you fare well."

She planted a kiss on the ragchild's brow, then pinched its soft wrists together and brought both its mittened hands down to Gercina's vagina.

Cloth ravelled inward between Gercina's labia as if through a wringer run in reverse.

Soon the soft head of the ragbaby hit the vaginal inlet, was compressed, folded, and drawn inside without much distension. Woven torso followed.

Soon only a lone cloth foot kicked, and the anti-loom of Gercina's body inhaled completely the warp and weft of her new embryo.

Gercina's midriff had begun to bloat and swell at the start of the process. Now it boasted the titanic rondure and everted navel of a woman within days of delivery. Kerry rubbed the outward measure of the woman's robust pregnancy soothingly with circular rhythms, and the massage sent Gercina irresistibly into slumber.

"Cook and cohere for a short time, my little Bloodchild. Grow your white bones, and don your black flesh. Let your heart hang from ribs no longer linen and a brain reside in your skull that has hardened to something more durable than a diaper. Then emerge like any newborn, the spawn of your adopted mother, and forget me forever."

Clad once more in her mannish garb, Kerry hopped out the window like a jackrabbit as dawn bustled in.

Hours passed filled with only deep breathings from the sleeping husband and wife. Galeno was first to awake. He found Gercina lying on her side, her back to him.

Galeno dropped a hand on her shoulder. "Gercina, look at the daylight. It must be very late. We should be up."

Gercina rolled over, a whale breaching. Her tranquil face reflected the accomplishment of a lifelong dream. Galeno, however, fell back in astonishment, momentarily mute.

"Cannot a mother-to-be rest abed a little longer?"

"Father of Christ! What have I done?"

"Only what I asked you. Here, put your hand on my stomach. Can you feel how strongly our little son kicks?"

* * *

Shaking his head in rueful wonderment, Arlindo Quincas emerged onto the broad and crowded shrub-shielded porch that wrapped The Blue Afternoon Hotel. Failing to respond to the hails from passing friends and employees and fellow businessmen, thus earning looks of curiosity, bafflement and quick affront, the man propelled his solid body directly toward the table where his five pards were wont to sit. At this postprandial hour, the men were just picking clean the remnants of a platter of goat ribs. The pile of greasy bones assembled before each man seemed somehow emblematic of each eater.

Tubby Ivo boasted the largest heap.

Senior member Ricardo had aligned all his neatly nibbled scraps in serried ranks.

Gnarly Estevao's portion showed only desultory toothmarks, as much meat remaining as bone.

The musteline Januario had left his debris jumbled as if by a hasty hyena.

Callow Belmiro had built a mock pagoda with his leftovers.

Quincas descended on the sated feasters like a maritime squall which suddenly lost all its energy upon striking land. The obviously perplexed hotel owner collapsed into a vacant chair and became the immediate focus of the quintet's attentions.

"What ails you, friend?" "Buck up, chum. Things cannot be as dreadful as your face portends!" "My compliments to the chef! This rack of goat was superb!" "Will you take a drink with us, Arlindo?" "Is it the bruja again, Arlindo?"

Only to the last two queries did Quincas respond, first by accepting a frosty glass, and then by nodding his head glumly and answering, "Yes, I think Senhorita Yemana has shown her hand once more."

Quincas recounted the crazy tale his bartender had related to him upon showing up for the start of his liquor-dispensing stint. His listeners nodded sagely or marvelingly throughout the account. When Quincas had finished, they ventured various comments and questions.

"So Galeno failed to get his wife to reveal what really happened during the night while he slept?" asked Januario. "I would have beat the truth out of her!"

Ricardo offered, "Such spontaneous quickenings are not unheard of in nature. It is said that a horsehair left in a stagnant puddle will become a species of worm overnight."

"Why do you suspect the presence of your bruja in this affair?" Belmiro wondered. "Do you have any proof?"

"No, of course not," answered Quincas. "Galeno never even mentioned her. But the similarity between the two events leads me to make the obvious connection. New arm, instant baby—who else could it be? Surely pitiful Galeno had nothing to do with this astounding conception, after so many barren years."

Ivo patted his own protuberant stomach fondly. "I must steer clear of your old mistress, Arlindo. I cannot afford to host a pregnancy atop this already sizable gut!"

After the laughter ceased, Ricardo said, "What now, Arlindo? Do you propose to search the Catshead for your quondam lover?"

"No, she has surely departed that neighborhood. She owns a restless soul, I tell you. Who can predict where she will turn up next?"

"Maybe in your bed," Januario said.

"He should be so lucky," Belmiro jibed. "No, the only sex our host can be assured of enjoying is when he accompanies us to the fabled, fragrant house of Senhora Graca this very Friday."

Quincas moaned dismally. "And right *there* is *another* problem." Quincas lowered his voice and looked around before speaking further. "I have received an invitation from Senhor Reymoa for that very same night. Darciana is being presented to society at his estate."

Ivo teasingly admonished, "Ah, you would rather attend a boring function for adolescents and their withered mothers than accompany us to enjoy the carnal affections of a bevy of hot beauties fresh off the boat from Three Lakes, where they grow the most seductive women. Ladyfingers and gingerbeer, rather than tail and booze. And all because your gangster host has a bank account totaling millions of claws."

"Not to mention," added Januario, "that any affront to Ovid Reymoa generally results in the loss of some part a man would rather keep."

"That is precisely the heart of my quandary! I do not care to waste my Friday among a pack of students and their chaperones, but I do not dare slight Reymoa! Why, even attending his affairs is no guarantee of his good will. What should I do, my friends? What should I do?"

Silent until now, the lean-faced Estevao spoke.

"The plight of our friend reminds me of an incident that happened during the time of my grandfather. Perhaps recounting it would help clarify his situation.

"At that period there resided in Bahia a man named Sinval Tomoz. My grandfather often spoke of him, both because Tomoz was his banker, and because of the bizarre events that happened to the respectable gentleman.

"Like many of us, Tomoz kept a mistress. But his wife was very hard-hearted about such a useful and common practice, and, without directly accusing her husband of any unfaithfulness, sought by every stratagem to deny him any extensive time with his young plaything. Errands galore descended on the shoulders of our hapless Tomoz, social obligations and travel invariably obtruded, and he managed to see his charming mistress barely once a week.

"Naturally, Tomoz found this situation incredibly frustrating. In vain he searched for a standard solution from the bag of tricks used by unfaithful husbands since time began, but came up short each time. Finally, he decided to turn to magic.

"At the time—as perhaps Ricardo, our oldest member, might barely recall from his childhood—no shop was complete without a lifesized effigy of an indio in front of its entrance. Each carved wooden indio would bear some token of the goods for sale inside, of course—a bundle of cigars, a skillet, a bolt of cloth. Before the advent of radio, such were the primitive methods by which our ancestors would advertise their wares, if you can credit it! In any case, Tomoz approached the most talented carver of such effigies with a strange request. He commissioned the man to sculpt an image of Tomoz himself, enjoining the artisan to render it as lifelike as possible.

"Well, the sculptor readily accepted the challenge, laboring for six months on his masterpiece and receiving a hefty sum for his work, as well as an enjoinment to utter silence on the matter. When the statue was finished, Tomoz loaded the stiff shrouded effigy, along with a spare set of clothing, into a cart and set out for the interior. There, he participated in a strange and secret and not undemanding ceremony led by an indio sorcerer who, to put a sharp point on it, brought the wooden Tomoz to life.

"Under cover of darkness, Tomoz and his double returned to the town. The cart drew up outside the mansion inhabited by Tomoz and his wife—they had no children—and Tomoz sent his handmade representative, now fully instructed in his duties, inside in his place. With all eagerness, Tomoz hied himself to the arms of his mistress.

"This routine succeeded wonderfully for several weeks. Each day the mock Tomoz would, as instructed, set out for work, to be met by the original Tomoz not far from the house, where the cheating banker would then hide the sensible dummy in a convenient locked woodshed. All would have doubtlessly proceeded without a hitch for years, had not some rascally children broken the lock on the woodshed and accidentally freed the dummy during the day.

"Out on his own for the first time, the false Tomoz went not back to the mansion, but somehow, perhaps sharing the memories of Tomoz, found his way to the apartment of the mistress.

A MOUTHFUL OF TONGUES

"That evening, the original Tomoz went to retrieve his stand-in, and found an empty shed instead. Flabbergasted and alarmed, Tomoz first went home to feed his wife some tale. It was the first time he had seen her since the era of deceit had been initiated. He found her waiting for him on the doorstep. She threw her arms around his neck and stuck her tongue in his ear! 'Oh, Sinval, I can hardly wait to get you in bed again tonight!'

"Needless to say, this was not the kind of reception Tomoz generally enjoyed from his wife. He disengaged himself, disbursed some kind of fable about a crisis at the bank, and, a painful intuition trembling in his gut, took off for the place of his mistress.

"Bursting into the love nest, he found his mistress kneeling like a dog, squealing obscenities she never employed with him, all the while being boned from behind by the unnatural Tomoz. Tomoz the man grabbed the shoulder of his double and pulled him off the woman. Then the penis of the living statue stood revealed. Soft-skinned yet perpetually hard as lignum vitae, the dick was a monstrous baton any woman would have killed for! An homage by the obsequious sculptor, no doubt, yet how the tribute had redounded against his patron!

"Well, once the astonished mistress received an explanation of this odd mixup, she expressed her immediate preference for the double! After administering a quite justifiable beating, Tomoz hastened home. He made a full confession and cast himself on the mercy of his spouse. Without saying a word, she ran out of the house. Exhausted, Tomoz slumped in a chair and poured himself a drink. Half an hour later, a runner brought the news that his wife and his mistress were engaged in a knockdown battle in the town square, all over the affections of the carven Tomoz!

"Tomoz shrugged, and merely said, 'If my double is man enough for both, let him have them.'

"This Solomonic message was conveyed to the battling women, who immediately ceased their quarrel, began to weep, and swore eternal fealty to each other through their tears. With the grinning substitute Tomoz, they gathered up various valuables for a grubstake and set out for a town on the far side of Bahia, where their scandalous story would be unknown."

Upon the completion of Estevao's lurid tale, his listeners sat stunned. Finally, Quincas said, "What is the lesson of such an uncanny recital, Estevao? Are you recommending that I churn up such a monster to stand proxy for me on Friday?"

"Of course not. I was simply trying to illustrate the dangers one encounters when he tangles with the supernatural. If you had not taken the bruja to bed in the first place, you would not have fallen under the purview of Senhor Reymoa, you would not have received an invitation to that party of that vain witch, Darciana, and you would be all set to accompany us to the innocent pleasures of the brothel."

"Always you blame Senhorita Yemana, who blessed me with this new arm! I should use it to smash your wizened face—"

Ricardo intervened. "Come, come, my friends! The solution is simplicity itself! This party for children must needs end by early evening, whereas the joyful carnal ruckus at the house of Graca will barely be getting underway by midnight. Attend the affair Reymoa invited you to, Arlindo, then join us afterwards for the real fun."

Quincas seemed struck by this notion. "Why not? How blind I was! I can satisfy everyone in turn!"

His friends clapped him on the back congratulatorily, except for Estevao, whose gloomy postscript was: "Precisely this phrase has many an overconfident fellow uttered, just before tumbling headlong into the pit."

* * *

The toylike ascending car of the funicular railway, painted brightly in tones of yellow, red and orange, clanked past its descending twin at the midpoint of the mammoth hill that bore on its exclusive green flanks a choice collection of rich estates, like exotic canapes on a bed of plain lettuce. An excess of riders stood on the car's running boards, clinging to brass handrails and eyeing enviously those who had been lucky enough to claim a seat inside. Despite some exceptions, a clear distinction between the groups prevailed: those inside seemed mostly to be household servants, dressed in servile finery, while those who chanced a tumble wore the more rugged gear demanded of gardeners, stable-boys, hewers of wood, shovelers of coal, and laundresses.

The car docked at the top of the hill, latches engaging noisily in a possessive iron lovebite. The waiting downward riders, few in number at this early morning hour, clustered wearily some distance away on the platform, allowing their fellow workers to disembark. Hopping down first, the standees began to trickle off along the bosky, macaw-and-parrot-accented avenues leading to the demanding lawns, kitchens, flowerbeds and kennels of their employers. The seated riders emerged more slowly through the open accordion doors at front and rear that channeled them.

One young woman stepping firmly down stood out from her compatriots, if only for her uncommon red hair like a cataract of lava, twisted and pinned into a weighty bun. Her pellucid faintly olive skin contrasted with the muddier or swarthier complexions of her peers. Her amplitudinous body, a wealth of breast, hips, and stomach, upper arms fleshy as pears, conducted a silent yet vehement argument with the demure white uniform of a lady's maid concealing it. White lisle stockings disappeared inside solid black shoes, their cracked leather polished with obvious care.

Wearing a faint and distant smile, the redhead strode with an air of untroubled confidence through the shady curves and down long straight stretches of roadway framed alternately by pollarded jacarandas or sharp-leafed palms. Occasionally from behind tall wrought-iron fences came the bark of an overzealous guard dog. Nannies and governesses trundled or tugged their youthful charges down the slate sidewalks. Sanitation workers guided broom-and-shovel-racked nightsoil carts full of horse manure collected from the raked gravel streets. To all these workers the woman in white made polite hellos.

Finally she arrived at a spear-topped gate which bore a simple metal plaque declaring the manse beyond to be REYMOA HOUSE. The snout of a simple speaking-tube protruded between two bars of the fence, its attached pipe diving into the ground, presumably to resurface in the mansion. The woman brought her unpainted full lips close to the funnel and announced herself:

"Maura Colapietro, reporting for duty." She paused a moment, as if trying to summon up a fuller explanation, then added, "This is my first day of employment."

No answer emerged from the tube, but rather there appeared before too long a shuffling old gatekeeper, who unlocked the barrier with a big key the size of a small dog's paw, and wordlessly ushered Maura across the threshold and pointed her toward the servants' entrance.

Immediately beyond the innocuous door, Maura encountered an older woman clad in black. The matron's rigid bearing bespoke the martinet, and her scowling face was not flattered by the tidy yet incongruous grey hairs peppering her upper lip.

"Senhorita Colapietro, you are nearly late."

"I prefer to say precisely on time, Senhora Soares."

Soares bristled. "Our terms diverge too widely, you young snip, and my definitions must rule. From now on, you will arrive fifteen minutes before the start of your shift, so that I may assess your appearance."

"So my workday really begins not at eight, but at seven-forty-five. This means I will have to take a much earlier tram. Will I be paid extra?"

"Of course not! What impudence! This is what comes from giving a foreigner a job that a Bahian should have. Why, if Senhorita Darciana had not approved your hiring herself, I would now be showing you my boot!"

Maura sought to mollify her supervisor. "Forgive me, Senhora Soares. I only sought clarification of the rules from the one who knows them best."

Soares snuffled her acceptance of the offered detente. "Put on your apron and gloves and begin polishing the silver which I have laid out in the pantry. But stay alert for a call from your mistress. Remember, the smallest whim expressed by Senhorita Darciana takes precedence over any other duty."

"To hear is to obey, Senhora."

Soares now seemed to recall her earlier expressed desire to judge Maura's garb. She eyed the young woman up and down before tendering a grudging approval. "Your uniform appears freshly laundered, and it seems you have actually bathed recently. But was there no more capacious clothing available? Your buttons are on the verge of popping!"

"This is the size I always wear."

"No doubt. And what of your hair? Do you dye it?"

"Certainly not."

"What kind of guinea has red hair?"

"My kind."

Apparently, Senhora Soares grew tired of banter when it did not trend in her favor. "Go on now, set about earning your pay."

Maura polished a sultan's worth of silver until eleven o'clock, wrinkling her nose at the sour chemical smell of the abrasive paste, before being summoned to the kitchen. There the dyspeptic, cigarette-smoking chef indicated a large silver tray heaped with cream-filled pastries and a stack of dishes, companioned with a smaller tray bearing a coffee pot, demitasse cups, creamer and sugar bowl.

"Senhorita Darciana demands her refreshment. The little princess is undergoing an excruciation worse than that of the martyrs, and needs some fortifying."

Maura dipped her finger into a bowl of leftover whipped cream and suckled what clung, stung lips pursing and relaxing. "Is she being tutored perhaps?"

The chef laughed. "Fat chance of that! Since her mother died, the daughter does whatever she pleases, and taking lessons is not on her short list of pleasures."

"What happened to Senhora Reymoa?"

Casting a furtive glance left and right, the chef replied, "This is not a subject wise people speak of."

"Oh. Fine. Can you tell me what the little princess *is* doing then?"

"Modeling last-minute alterations on her gown for the party tomorrow."

"And this counts as torture?"

"When you are Darciana it does. Now, can you carry both trays, or shall I fetch help?"

Maura hoisted first with two hands the heavier platter to shoulder level, shifting her purchase to its undercenter, then hoisted one-handed the lighter tray. The chef smiled broadly. "What muscles! Are your legs just as well-equipped?"

"What chance do you have of learning such a thing?" Maura answered with mock sternness belied by her acceptance of a pinch on her buttocks from the chef on her way out of the kitchen.

A curving, carpeted marble staircase led upward. Maura stepped carefully with her burdens. The second-floor corridor immediately reached at the head of the stairs led from front to back of the house. Maura walked with the assurance of one who possesses solid directions past many closed doors to the penultimate one. There she tapped as delicately as she could with the side of the toe of her shoe.

The voice that responded was adolescently girlish yet steely. "Enter."

"My hands are full. Could you open the door, please, Senhorita?"

"Mei-mei! Put down your pins and get that foolish door!"

Swinging open, the gaping door revealed not a young Bahian girl but a Chinawoman. Older than Maura yet not so old as Senhora Soares, the Oriental woman exhibited many alluring features commonly associated with her race: darkling canted eyes, cupids-bow incarnadined lips, skin dusty gold, long hair with a nigrescent sheen. She wore a fancifully embroidered azure silk dress featuring a slit up one side, and shoes with a significant elevation of heel.

Mei-mei stepped aside so that Maura could enter, then swung the door shut.

"Lock that damn door so we're not bothered again," ordered Darciana.

Maura turned from setting down her trays of refreshments on a carven sideboard to assess her mistress.

An enormous canopied bed occupied half the room, along with bureaus, wardrobes and a vanity. Darciana Reymoa stood on an overstuffed red velvet hassock in the middle of the bedroom, so that her head topped Maura's. Barefoot, she wore a one-piece ivory cotton undergarment that covered her from upper arm to mid-thigh. Pinched at the waist with a slip-knotted tie running through miniscule loops, the loose unitard fastened with lacing up the back. Beneath this prim covering, the lines of Darciana's body seemed yet untransfigured by time into full womanhood: mild bust, slim hips. Her bare legs showed a similar gracileness. Her shiny brown hair hung straight and dense halfway down her back, and her narrow, sharp-nosed face exhibited none of the pudgy smudging shown by her father's; although a similar obstinacy and fixity of purpose dwelled in her cool gaze and firm lips.

Next to Darciana stood a headless mannequin wearing the triumphal gown under construction, a satin confection of lace and bows. Mei-mei had already returned to her sartorial duties, nipping and tucking with needle and thread.

"Pour me a coffee, Maura, and bring it to me."

"How do you take it, Senhorita?"

"As the Arabs do, hot, black and sweet."

Maura sugared the coffee as instructed, and handed the saucered cup over to her mistress. Maintaining eye-contact with her newest servant, Darciana sipped deeply. Cup clinked into china cradle, and Darciana said, "Mei-mei, I will step down now. I deserve a break from your tyranny."

The Oriental seamstress nodded, but made no reply, and Darciana hopped off the hassock. Standing on the floor, she was a head shorter than the other two women, yet an unshakable imperiousness far in advance of her age caused her to seem to tower over them both.

"So, Maura, how do you like your first day on the job?"

"Very well, thank you, Senhorita. Although Senhora Soares is a real dragon."

"You need not worry about that withered bitch, as long as you stay in my favor. Laudalina Soares owes everything to my father, and knows enough not to risk my displeasure. Papa rescued her from utter poverty years ago, when her husband was murdered by some of the rivals Papa once struggled against, before he exterminated them all during the great struggles over the gold fields of Minas Gerais."

"A sad story."

"Indeed. Our large hearts make Papa and I very susceptible to the sufferings of lesser folks. Why, I myself have already begun a similar career of rescuing unfortunates. Take Mei-mei for instance." Darciana directed a keen gaze toward the Chinese woman, who continued fussing with the dress. "Back in her native Cathay, she became an orphan during the unpleasantness with the Boxers. Missionaries rescued her from the chaos and relocated her and her fellow foundlings to Bahia. But all did not go well for poor Mei-mei. Due either to outside pressures or from inward inclinations, she took up whoring. Is that not so, Mei-mei?"

Impassive, the seamstress looked up from her work and nodded.

"I learned of her plight through my brothers. Hermeto and Getulio. Have you met them yet?"

"No, Senhorita."

"Ah, you will, soon enough. In any case, once I became aware of Mei-mei and her plight, I determined to effect a transformation. I had her contract purchased away from the whorehouse and apprenticed her to a tailor for a year. Now she is my private couturier."

"A very charitable deed, Senhorita."

"Yes, I thought so too. And your own case awakened similar feelings in me, although of course you were not faring quite so poorly as Mei-mei."

"It is true. For one so young, I have taken my share of hard knocks in a rough and tumble existence."

Darciana finished her coffee and handed the cup and saucer back to her maid. Her fingertips maintained contact with Maura's for an unnatural length of time beneath the saucer before she relinquished the drained cup, undissolved stained sugar sludging the bottom.

"Pirates, though!" Darciana let a patently exaggerated shiver quake her shoulders. "Tell me again what happened."

Without reserve, Maura recounted her early disastrous career. "I was only a child of twelve, the daughter of a poor fisherman and his wife in Brindisi, when I was stolen away by the Turkish pirates who slaughtered my parents and every other villager. For years those stinking bearded ruffians used me harshly, a veritable plaything for all their lusts, as they traveled about the Mediterranean in their circuit of rape and pillage. Putting in at the Azores, they finally met their deserved end, under the guns of a Portuguese dreadnought. With nothing left for me back in Brindisi, I took ship to Bahia. Once here, I supported myself with many odd jobs, the last of which you saw me at, filleting fish at the market, employing the skills I had been taught in my youth."

"So you feel a proper debt to my charity, no doubt?"

"But of course."

"I am gratified to hear you say so. Refill my cup, Maura, and pour one for yourself and Mei-mei as well."

A MOUTHFUL OF TONGUES

"Thank you, Senhorita. Mei-mei, how will you have yours?"

Darciana replied for the seamstress. "She takes it light, no sugar, as she would tell you herself, had not the savage Boxers deprived her of her tongue. Show our new friend your lack, Mei-mei."

The beautiful Chinese woman obediently opened her mouth: glistening pink cavern with no agile carpeting tenant. Maura stared with frank interest and no visible apprehension, as if accustomed to sights far worse, until the other woman brought her lips together again in a sad smile.

"This disfigurement left poor Mei-mei unable to perform certain duties connected with her old trade, but she certainly learned to compensate, as her exemplary record of earnings testified."

Mei-mei ceased her labors to accept her coffee. Maura asked, "Do you ever extend a helping hand to the indios, Senhorita?"

Darciana nearly spat. "Those filthy savages! Of course not! I restrict my sympathy to the civilized races."

Maura adjusted the proportions of her own beverage. For a time the three women, seated on various chairs, sipped wordlessly. Then Darciana spoke:

"This brew is strong! Sweat is coursing my chest! You two must be suffering likewise. Mei-mei, I give you permission to adopt a more informal look."

Mei-mei stood up and reached behind herself to unbutton her sheathlike dress. In moments it crumpled around her heeled feet. The honeyed skin of the ex-whore shone radiantly everywhere save where a silk bandeau shielded her moderately full breasts and where a pair of loose step-ins cloaked her loins.

Darciana's eyes glittered. "Now you, Maura."

"But what of the propriety demanded by my humble status? Can it be right for me to chance being discovered in such a state?"

"My word is law here, Maura. And your job consists in obeying me."

Maura seemed not overly troubled, as if her protest had been merely *pro forma*. "As you say, Senhorita."

Stripped to a merrywidow-style undergarment whose garters upheld her stockings, Maura's lush body anchored the far end of the somatic spectrum on which

Mei-mei occupied the middle and Darciana the immature end. Maura's whalebone circumflexure terminated just below her navel, revealing her carroty-amber bush unconcealed by any pants.

"Now I feel more at ease," Darciana said. "After all, I was partially unclothed in front of you both already. That is no condition for a mistress—unless of course she is sharing her nudity with her servants. Maura, would you fetch us the pastry now?"

Maura stepped across the room to the sideboard, the tantalizing motion of her solid comfortable ass cheeks mapping each step. She returned with the platter of cream pastry. Darciana selected an eclair, brought the long stuffed bun to her lips and flicked a tonguetip's worth of eggy filling from its open end.

"So like a cock, do you not agree, ladies? Mei-mei, take off your step-ins and lift one foot up to my old perch."

Black-haired cunt unjacketed, one shod foot planted firmly on the floor beside the hassock, Mei-mei raised the other to dimple with heel the hassock's velvet top. Still bearing the eclair, a bright-eyed Darciana moved to kneel before her seamstress.

"Open your twat for this crusty cock, you sweet whore."

Mei-mei reached down to spread her labia and enlarge her hole. Maura moved instinctively closer for a more detailed view, her breathing accelerando. Darciana inserted the eclair shallowly into Mei-mei's cunt, and began to gently work it deeper with parity-preserving half-twists: the rich stripe of outer chocolate smeared Mei-mei's labia. When the pastry was two-thirds concealed, Darciana advised, "Get ready for his cum, Mei-mei."

Butting her palm against the exposed end of the eclair, Darciana squeezed until the pastry crumpled.

An uncouth mute's sound escaped Mei-mei as the ice-box-cooled custard flowed into her. Darciana removed the squashed pastry and took a long lick off the end that had been buried. A syrup of cunt lubricant, chocolate and custard slicked her mouth, and a sprinkle of crumbs collected in the corners of her lips. The mistress of Reymoa House turned to Maura, who had freed her breasts from the corset cups and begun playing with them. Her fat nipples erected readily.

"Your turn, you randy little guinea. Lie on the rug."

A MOUTHFUL OF TONGUES

Maura dropped to the carpet, and, feet flat and knees bent, exposed her already dripping cunt, unique phoenix in its nest of flames. Darciana selected a second pastry and simulated another ejaculation.

"Now both of you must get every last drop of cum out. Maura, you will really have to exert what I could tell are some superb cunt muscles to help poor Mei-mei reach it all. But of course, although there is only one tongue between you, you both have your fingers."

The Reymoa girl arranged the kneeling Mei-mei above the recumbent Maura until the women had assumed the requisite intimacy, Mei-mei's legs buttressing the cathedral of Maura's ribs. Mei-mei's bandeau had ridden down to expose her sunset-nippled breasts.

"Begin now, and leave not a trace behind."

Positioning her spectator's face close to Mei-mei's ass, Darciana intently watched Maura's tongue groove the Chinese woman's cunt, dip within her hole, and emerge coated in factitious cum.

"Oh, that was well done for a start!" Darciana shifted herself south along the clasping women and told Mei-mei, "Here, allow me to instruct you in the proper technique."

Darciana stuck her middle finger to the last knuckle up Maura's cunt, then withdrew it slimed. She pushed her finger into Mei-mei's mouth, and the Oriental's lips skimmed all the sweetness off during the digit's slow withdrawal.

Now the two women engaged in *soixante-neuf* began to lap and probe each other's fleshy desserts with increasing abandon. Darciana peered intently from every angle, from time to time aiding verbally or manually. But the youngest woman did not stimulate her own cunt, seemingly intent on remaining in possession of her composure so as to orchestrate the licking and fingering.

As Mei-mei and Maura neared their fullest expression of pleasure, Darciana swiftly retrieved a sewing needle from her seamstress's kit. She positioned herself above Mei-mei's rump and pricked the woman's ass with the needle. Mei-mei croaked a shocked unintelligible vocable, but did not cease plumbing Maura's twat. A drop of blood tiny as an insect's eye manifested on the Oriental's golden skin.

"The pirates have you now, girls. Put on a good show, and they might let you live."

As much from their own desire to crescendo as from Darciana's stagy threat, the women redoubled their sucking. Darciana continued randomly to puncture Mei-mei's ass, until it was stippled with blood. Coalescing in a few places, the blood rivuleted down Mei-mei's epidermal slopes to her inner thighs.

"Lick it off, Maura."

Eyes wide open to catch those of her mistress, Maura sopped crimson tracks with her sugar-coated tongue.

The two women came explosively with paired shrieks and grunts. Mei-mei collapsed atop Maura, and the two breathed heavily for a few moments before rolling apart.

Darciana stood over the exhausted women in a regal stance, arms crossed over her small bosom.

"Let us pleasure *you* now, Senhorita," Maura offered with an apparently genuine generosity.

Darciana's voice was all harshness. "Forget that. I have other resources in that regard. I want nothing more from you two now than to clean yourselves up and tidy my room. Make sure no blood stains that carpet! If I see so much as a single spot, you will both receive a chastisement that will astound you."

Still clad only in her one-piece undergarment, Darciana left her bedroom. Out in the hall, she swiftly padded to a set of double doors. From the rightmost one projected a big brass handle, and Darciana levered that door open and slipped inside, pausing just inside the room.

The library of Reymoa House, two stories tall, was a cavernous room with polished floor, its wheel-laddered shelves—filled with uniformly bound editions shamefully hiding their uncut pages—rising to the ornate plaster-work ceiling; a marble-topped reading table, a lectern supporting an open Bible, and several leather chairs patterned with square nail-heads along their perimeters occupied the oval-carpeted center of the space.

In two of the closely placed high-backed chairs, buttery drinks handy to reach, puffing with nearly obscene contentment on aromatic cigars, sat two young and handsome clean-shaven men, certainly no older than twenty-five. Very close in age, perhaps only a year apart, they exhibited brotherly affinities of feature—granitic chins, prominent cheekbones, blue eyes—although the hair of one was ashen-blonde, while the other's was closer to dusky sorrel.

Arguing spiritedly between puffs, the men remained unaware of their visitor for a moment, until the lighter-haired one spotted Darciana through the obscuring wreaths of bluish smoke.

"Hermeto! Little sister favors us with her charming presence, just in time to mediate our disagreement!"

"As usual, Getulio, your inspiration races ahead of mine! Darciana, dear, please join us."

Smiling like an usurer about to foreclose a property, Darciana sashayed over to her brothers. She dropped down onto Hermeto's lap and threw her arms around his neck. She lifted her legs and placed her feet in Getulio's lap. The brothers laughed. Securing his drink from its perch, Hermeto tipped the tumbler's rim to Darciana's lips and she took a mouthful of the potent rum, swirled it around inside her cheeks, then gulped. Getulio leaned forward to swipe crumbs from the crevices of Darciana's smile.

"Feasting on sweets again, sister?"

"Oh, yes, let me tell you all about it—"

Hermeto raised a peremptory hand. "One moment. You have to negotiate our dispute first. Getulio, the newspaper, please."

Getulio took from the table a copy of the *Messenger of the North* already folded open to the day's racing schedule and handed it to his brother, commenting, "You know I am not much of a one for imaginary stories, brother, but I must direct your attention to the one featured in the *Messenger* today. Something called 'She Beast,' and a very odd little nightmare it is. I venture to predict this fellow Sabino will make his name with this gem."

"I might read it in due time, brother, if nothing more pressing intervenes." Hermeto held the paper before Darciana and stabbed a line with his forefinger. "Now, pay close attention, sister. We intend to wager a thousand claws on the first race today at the Sambadrome. But my younger sibling insists on backing a nag improbably called 'Chocolate Woman,' while I in my elder wisdom want to support 'Carnival Queen.' Since he is just as inflexible as I, you will have to decide."

"'Chocolate Woman.'"

Hermeto made as if to eject Darciana from his lap, causing her to shriek and hold on more tightly. "Traitorous girl! Did he share his drink with you, or did I? Oh, well, I suppose I will have to abide by your capricious judgment. Is there any rational basis for your decision?"

"An auspicious omen, rather. I have just tasted the twats of two women all smeared with chocolate."

A different light than gaming's radiance sparked in the eyes of the two men. "You must tell us all about it." "Yes, do not spare a single detail."

Darciana began to narrate the carnal encounter she had engineered between her servants. Beneath her small massaging feet, Getulio's trouser-bound cock swiftly hardened, as did Hermeto's prick pinned beneath her ass. The brothers relinquished their drinks and smokes, so that Getulio could run his hands up and down her legs, and Hermeto could plump her breasts.

Darciana finished her account: "And I daresay that Maura will soon show both of you randy bastards as much hot cunt as Mei-mei already has."

"Ah," said Hermeto, "but both lovely ladies are tired out now, thanks to you, and only you are here."

He began to unlace the back of her undergarment, while Getulio slipped the knot of her waist cord. Soon Darciana stood naked, her hirsute mound in contrast to breast buds still pink-tipped.

The brothers doffed their light woollen trousers with all speed, revealing mirrored cocks that further validated their consanguinity, and now all three siblings were standing. Darciana leaned back against Hermeto, but her relative shortness left his cock in the small of her back. She swung her crook'd arms toward him, he brought his forward, and they locked at the elbows. He lifted her effortlessly off her feet until his cock furrowed her cunt deeply, like a fencerail. Darciana closed her eyes and moaned. Projecting well beyond Darciana's slim body, the penis seemed to issue from her own flesh.

Getulio kneeled before the conjoined genital assemblage. Darciana raised her legs to drape them over his shoulders, and he reached a hand to cup Hermeto's balls.

"Do not be angry with me, big brother, because little sister decided the horse for our wager in my favor. You know both she and I would do anything for you."

A MOUTHFUL OF TONGUES

Blue-shadowed lips circled the head of Hermeto's cock. Getulio swallowed inches of his brother's dick until stopped by Darciana's splayed cunt. He worked his upper lip as best he could against her clit while squeezing Hermeto's balls. Withdrawing his lips back down the cock, Getulio favored the glans with the attentions of his tongue for a time while thumbing Darciana's clit.

Eventually, both the standing man and the girl he carried could tolerate no more foreplay. The kneeling Getulio rose up with Darciana's legs sliding down to encircle his waist. Getulio clasped her narrow ass and pulled her away some degrees from Hermeto. Hermeto bent at the knees slightly to slide his wet cock up the cozy portal of Darciana's ass. Getulio's matching dick filled her cunt, a hole nearly as tight.

The trio held still for a moment, until Darciana's noisy squirmings triggered synchronized plungings from front and rear. Ballsack knocked ballsack, twin pendulums measuring the duration of their ecstasy. Sweat and juices slathered the intricate machine comprised of the three sets of genitals.

Hermeto, favored by both mouth and ass, came first, gushing deep up Darciana; Getulio lasted a mere minute longer.

Tripartite engine now discomposed into separate components, Darciana instantly adopted a spraddle-legged stance and beckoned the men.

"Hurry, hurry, boys! Do I have to tell you what I want after all this time!"

Now swapping their former womanly niches, Getulio kneeled at his sister's asshole, and Hermeto likewise commanded her cunt. Darciana placed a hand on top of each head, gripped tightly locks of contrasting hair, and pushed their faces more deeply against her flesh. The brothers began to recover with their mouths what each other had loaned with their cocks.

"Everyone else thinks only your hair distinguishes you. But Darciana knows better! The flavors of your cums is so distinct! Go ahead, suck it all out and tell me if I lie!"

* * *

Inaccessible to the public, the fifth floor of The Blue Afternoon Hotel featured a warren of abbreviated rooms with slanted ceilings mimicking the exterior mansard roof. The not unpleasant smell of a forgotten lumberhouse permeated the entire labyrinth—insect generations; the subtle alchemic compounds born in a crucible lit by the slow, cold fire of time, where wood was transmuted to dust; remnants of aromatic barks still clinging to shaved planks—and the few venturesome breezes that found their way in through small round windows (which from the street outside looked like a row of portholes on a ship) did little to dispel a solemn mortuary closeness.

In a room no way exceptional from any other on this level, Arlindo Quincas was performing his grooming rituals before a spotted looking-glass. An iron bedstead, a dresser, a pitcher and basin, a chamberpot, a chifferobe: the hotel employees who inhabited this warren would have felt completely at home in the owner's simple room.

Quincas applied pomade to hair and mustache, and took a military-style handleless brush to his coiffure. He poured a finger of warm water into a glass, swished it around in his mouth, then spat into the basin. He donned the new suit jacket that matched his dove-grey trousers, then hitched fussily at the shoulder of the sleeve that covered his new arm, as if, despite appearances, he were convinced, through long mental and physical accommodation to his old amputation, that somehow the jacket hung asymmetrically.

The loud invariable metronoming of a wind-up clock fought the silence of this aeyrie. Radium-outlined dial read six o'clock. Painterly light embellishing the rim of the porthole window slanted so as to indicate a westering sun.

Someone knocked at Quincas's door. He sighed, like a man who balks feebly at the perpetual demands of a high undischargeable position. Composing his face in lines of right-minded responsibility, he strode to the door and opened it.

As if carved by the master sculptor from Estevao's story of the randy effigy and placed before Quincas's door by a prankster, there stood an indio and india, faces as imperturbable as the moon's.

"Ixay, Yeena—what brings you here at this hour?"

The aboriginal gardener and indigenous barmaid both blinked with slow deliberateness, and then Ixay spoke.

A MOUTHFUL OF TONGUES

"We must leave your employment for a time, Senhor."

Quincas shook his head as if the words defied sense. "What? What kind of foolish talk is this? Have I mistreated you? Have any of the guests trespassed on your dignity? If so, name them, and they will be gone!"

Ixay regarded Yeena as if perhaps she might like to speak, but she only bowed her head. "No," said the gardener, "nothing of that nature. You are a good boss, Senhor. The difficulty arises elsewhere. We have just received word from our headman, Xingu, ordering us to return to our village this very night. There is trouble abroad in the land, and all the tribe must be present to deal with it."

"My friends, I do not understand any of this. But I see you are both fully determined to depart. Let me stipulate that your positions remain open indefinitely. Return at any time—as soon as possible, in fact. Damn, but I will be hard-pressed to fill your spots on such short notice! And the cattle-drovers arrive in town soon—"

"We are sorry, Senhor. But it cannot be helped."

"Well, let us go down to the office, and I will settle up your pay."

"Please keep our pay in trust for us, Senhor. Where we are going, money has no value."

Shortly after the pair of natives had left for their obscure tribal reunion (latent aroma of cigar smoke, fading clicking of cunt jewelry), small leather packs strapped to their backs, Quincas too descended to the street. A boy brought his brace of horses and trap around and Quincas clambered aboard and took the reins.

At the foot of the towering hill where the richest citizens dwelled, in a leafy neighborhood known as Ambergris Bottoms, where merchants and tradesmen kept their dignified homes, Quincas pulled up before a modest house. A curtain twitched at a window, and then the front door opened. A silver-haired, snow-bearded man who might have been cousin to the quintet's sobersided Ricardo emerged with a woman of his own age. The householders kissed, and then the man hastened to join Quincas, who gee'd up the horses once his passenger was settled.

"Arlindo, all my thanks for sharing your conveyance! My own horse will relish the rest. A doctor's mare knows many sleepless nights."

"My pleasure, Flávio. It is good to have company when visiting Senhor Reymoa. Alone, I might have turned around halfway there and gone back to my simple bachelor pleasures."

"Ah, let us not allow the hyberbolic reputation that has fastened itself to Ovid Reymoa prevent us from enjoying his drink and food. There will be many of our friends there, and we need not associate overmuch with the Reymoa clan and their sycophants once we have made an obligatory bow or two in their direction, and complimented the little Senhorita on her pubescent charms."

"Still, I feel a vague unease—"

"Oh, put aside such ridiculous presentiments. They are invariably wrong! Let me give you an example. Just last night, I received on my porch your very own bartender, Galeno, in an extremely distressed state. 'Doctor, come quickly, my wife is giving birth!' On the way to the Catshead, I asked whether the pregnancy had been at all abnormal. 'How should I know? We have not seen a doctor till now. There just was no time.' Imagine, nine months the Lord gives us to prepare, and this man claims not to have found a single minute to bring his expectant wife to a doctor! I can see a farmer in the interior making such an excuse, but the educated inhabitant of a modern city— A shame, really! So you can imagine that I really anticipated the worst. Instead, what did I experience? The smoothest delivery I ever attended. I was more witness than actor. That baby practically climbed out of the womb! A real little black devil he was, perfectly formed in every limb, and suckling like a soldier before I left for my bed."

Quincas pondered this tale, as if ruminating on facts unknown to Doctor Zefiro. "Galeno, a father. After all these years, who would have guessed he had it in him? I expect I shall have to raise his pay a claw or two." Quincas clucked his tongue. "Still, Doctor, you must admit that once in a while a hunch comes true."

"Not tonight, Arlindo, surely. What could go wrong at such a well-planned party?"

By switchbacks and steep ascents the laboring horses brought the men to the open gates of Reymoa House, just as a confectioner sunset was glazing the skies. The moon, a day past full, had begun to contest the sun's dominion. Numerous carriages, all more elegant than Quincas's, lined the drive, many still discharging passengers. A liveried equerry held the reins of their trap while Quincas and Flávio descended with as much dignity as possible. They turned to face the impressive mansion, hulking like some antique fossil giant quarried from the sediments of the ages.

Without warning, as though out of the gates of hell, through the open front door and down the mansion's front stairs burst a pack of screaming people, guests mingled indiscriminately with servants. A taffeta-gowned dowager tripped and was heedlessly trampled, a child in velvet short-pants fell but was snatched up by a man in formal wear, a girl who was plainly one of Darciana's peers became entangled in her own petticoats, spun like a top and toppled.

Quincas's jaw hung open like a lobster trap: for impressively dismaying as the human exodus was, the pale oceanic surge of strange gelatinous liquid, billowy and lunar, that chased the partyers out the door like a pack of lazy amoebic tigers some feet behind its quarry was more strangely alarming still.

* * *

Over and over like a monomaniacal and tireless lover, the romantically uninventive yet persistent sea tongued the sand, depositing spittle-like spume on the sandy bubbling bosom of its unresponsive mate. A grounded dory notched the same beach—mast stowed, nets and floats bundled neatly—and a perfume with keynotes of iodine, tar, and unscavenged fish-offal graced the air. Civic architect for a realm of dreams, the full moon engineered a broad highway across the ocean's flooded fazendas.

A wavery line of seawrack defined the beach's highwater mark: many kinds of desiccated marine flora, empty shells, the crisp memory of a jellyfish, rare bits of polished driftglass, topaz, azure or alizarine.

In the dry sands above this festooned border, a person, apparently homeless, had formed themselves a shallow nest for sleeping. Shoeless, dressed in male clothing, the sleeper lay curled on one side, face cradled in bent arm.

Closely around the sleeper in the sandy depression, dozens of living crabs had arrayed themselves. Motionless save for the slight stir of an eyestalk or pincer, their wet yet dangerously drying shells catching the moonlight, the crabs outlined the shape of the sleeper like a caricaturist's thick charcoal lines. As if on guard or paying tribute, they maintained their vigil over the sleeper through several hundred slow and peaceful breaths.

Some distance further from the water, the beach metamorphosed into a line of small dunes spiked with grass. A path between nearby dunes showed a line of footprints that led to the sleeper. Now down this path crept three men, ruffians all, bearing truncheons and rope. Earrings glinted in the silver spew of the moon.

Stealthily exiting the dunes, the men instantly spotted the sleeper and rushed as swiftly and as quietly as possible across the pocketing sands, trampling and scattering the guardian crabs. Two thugs fell on their victim, while the third viciously but expertly clubbed the sleeper's head across the occipital. Wood cracked bone, and their victim jerked galvanically, then went limp.

"Is it her?" asked the leader.

One kneeling man lit a wooden match with the scratch of a thumbnail, while his companion felt around beneath the unconscious woman's clothing before reporting, "Boobs and a cunt and the purple print from the ass of the devil across her cheek. She must be the one."

"Tie her up then, tight. Feet too."

Roped like a steer, the woman was hoisted up by two of the henchmen. With their leader going ahead, they carried her away, through the dunes and out of sight.

Left behind in the person-shaped sand bowl, a blot of blood remained. As if drawn to this relic of their goddess, the surviving crabs cautiously returned, keeping their distance. As they watched, the blood began to fulminate and boil with partial intelligence. The exmatriated molecules of transgenic hemoglobin and strange proteins, too puny to achieve motility, cohered and quested wildly about in place, frantic for the organic, yet encountering only sand, since, with instinctive wisdom, no crab ventured within range of the blood lassoes. Finally, exhausted, the benthic snippet collapsed in on itself, dying and swiftly decomposing.

The crabs decamped, and the impartial moon traced its nightly circuit over Bahia, shedding light without favoritism over slum and mansion, sinner and saint, the dead and the living.

A MOUTHFUL OF TONGUES

As always, dawn reached the crest of the oligarchs' hill first, gilding spires and diademing treetops. In the kitchens of Reymoa House, coffee was brewed, melons were sliced, muffins were toasted, and fat-flecked sausages grilled. Food collated onto plates, plates arrayed on wicker lap-rests, lap-rests graced with linen, silver and the morning edition of the *Messenger*, the breakfasts were dispatched to the various bedrooms of the Reymoa sire and scions. Then preparations among the scurrying servants for a much larger affair began. Fowls were plucked, fish gutted, shrimp peeled, and loaves molded; ovens accepted pastries and roasts, fruit punch was mixed, and roe-speckled canapes shaped like butterflies swarmed across vast platters.

In the rest of the mansion, other chores were underway: floral arrangements, ballroom decorations, party favors for the adolescent guests. The whole household seethed like an anthill covered with a spill of sugar.

Only the library seemed isolated from the activity. Its double doors remained firmly closed. And when Hermeto and Getulio ambled down the corridor around noon, plainly intent on a bout with liquor decanter and humidor, they found the library's locks uncustomarily engaged.

"This is passing odd," said the darker Hermeto, rattling the handle futilely. "Only the old boar himself could have ordered this room locked. But why?"

Getulio swiped a fair forelock off his brow. "Perhaps father has suddenly developed an interest in the classics. Maybe he is busy reading up on his namesake even as we speak."

"Ha! We will never live to see that day! No, I suspect something more in line with his usual seedy activities—extortion, bribery or embezzlement, say."

"One thing we can be certain of, he is not closeted with a woman!"

"Shh, you fool! Do you want the old fossil—"

The right-hand door swung open, framing the stern and unsmiling blade-kissed visage of Ovid Reymoa. Nothing save a portion of shelving was visible beyond his immaculately suited and plug-like presence. The father regarded his sons with eyes blank as twin cenotaphs before speaking.

"What do you two fucking pansies want here?"

As elder, Hermeto answered. "Nothing, Senhor. It is only that we normally—"

"This is not a normal day. I am using the library today. Go elsewhere to conduct your debaucheries."

Getulio ventured a mild protest. "A fine cigar and a few fingers of rum hardly constitute debauchery, father."

Ovid Reymoa quirked his mouth in the thinnest of shark grins. "You should wipe the cunt juice of your sister off your face before you attempt to speak innocently of noble rum, boy. Listen to me now: I do not care what you two and Darciana do together. Better for her to exercise her hot tail here in the house than abroad, where my enemies might take advantage of her. That was the failing of your mother, remember? And unfortunately, Darciana seems to have the same insatiable cunt that Sonia owned—or which owned her. Anyway, who better for a Reymoa girl to fuck than one of her kindred? No, I do not object to any of your couplings. But do not deny them! The debaucheries that a man owns up to strengthen him. The ones he denies kill him. Get the hell out of here now! I have an important matter underway."

The door's instant, unannounced slamming caused the brothers to jump backwards. Recovering their composure, they both essayed brave yet nervous laughs, then, arms draped around each other's shoulders, strutted off.

On the far side of the door, Ovid Reymoa turned to contemplate the reason for his uncommon occupation of the library.

Stripped bare, unconscious, the foreign bruja slumped in a wing-backed chair, supported only by ropes around her torso and criss-crossing her breasts. Chance intersections of the lashings quilted her flesh into puffy parallelograms. Her head lolled, so that only a mere token of her purple satanic womb-blot showed, and her short black hair was crusted with dried sandy blood. Her hands, bound at their wrists, assumed a prayerful position atop the escutcheon of her pubic moss. Cords knotted about her ankles and knees completed her bondage.

Reymoa walked to the empty chair opposite his captive, and dropped his dense poundage into the observer's seat. On the table close to hand sat a full capless bottle of white rum and a half-sized crude homemade machete, the handle of the well-used big knife wrapped with sweat-stained leather.

A MOUTHFUL OF TONGUES

Reymoa gripped the bottle by its neck and slugged a draught directly from it. Spittle leashed lips to glass across part of its arc of removal. He socketed the bottle atop his gut, then settled back in his seat.

"Three more hours, witch. If you do not waken by then on your own, I will offer some incentives. I cannot spend all day here, no matter how important my schemes. My little girl has a party tonight, and her Papa must be there."

Louvering his eyes, Reymoa passed into the same kind of alert predatory lull that a bush-concealed hunting cat might exhibit. Now and again he drank from his bottle, smacking his lips with a peasant's primal pleasure.

The level in the bottle fell to one quarter, and the bruja still had not stirred. Save for her continued shallow breathing, she might have been dead. Reymoa pulled a pocket-watch out of his vest, consulted it, then stood without any apparent signs of inebriation. He picked up the machete and moved to hover over the bound woman. Upending his bottle, he doused her head with rum. The liquor trickled down her face and stingingly into her wound, but brought no reaction. Reymoa tossed the empty bottle partway across the room, where it thumped and rolled till it met the wall.

"All right, witch. You were warned."

A nipple, mashed between blunt thumb and forefinger's second knuckle, berried outward. The honed edge of the machete, a single overlooked mote of rust mottling its scoured steel, chorded areola's circumference, furrowing the tit without penetrating.

Reymoa sliced.

No blood flowed. The secret white ducted meat underlying the lost nipple churned, and rapidly gained structure. A replacement nipple bloomed and everted like timelapse photography of a flower unfurling, restoring seamless integrity to the rope-diamonded breast.

The bruja lifted her head and smiled. Her skyey irises seemed to sparkle, twin wellsprings centered around bottomless pupils. She did not struggle against her bonds.

"Do you know the power of what you have harvested there, Senhor? And how many more of my mammary crowns will you need? I suspect at least a second, if what I have heard about you is true."

Reymoa's face registered, first, shock, then a powerful remastery of self. He stepped backward toward the table.

111

Suddenly realizing he still held the pinch of unnatural flesh, he dropped the gobbet almost accidentally into a clean crystal ashtray upon the table's marble top.

"What—what have you heard about me, witch?"

"That you are a capon, no longer a real man."

Reymoa appeared to waver between the contradictory extremes of explosive wrath and abject shame, muscles in face and forearms twitching as if eager to respond to the affront, before finally speaking in a tone that mingled the two emotions. "You have heard true. Some years ago I was unmanned. Here, bitch, have a good look."

Loosed one-handedly, suitpants fell, and Reymoa stepped out of them, using his shoes uncaringly to extricate himself from the expensive fabric. The tails of an undershirt draped his genital area. This apron he lifted up.

A mangled remnant cock like a chewed pencil stubbed a scarred androgynous wasteland.

Reymoa said, "Seen enough? Possibly the last woman to gaze on this disaster was my wife. It was fresh then, for she was present when I lost my virility. But she lived only a few minutes longer than my balls. Would you care to hear the story? At least one listener has found it very instructive."

"You are the host, Senhor. Let it be as you wish."

Reymoa grinned. "Your bravado entertains me. But just remember that your life is at my disposal."

Still unabashedly pantless, hairy legs like temple pillars, Reymoa walked to the bar and secured another bottle of rum. He sliced open its seal with the everpresent machete and managed to unscrew the cap without relinquishing his knife. After consuming more of the potent drink, he returned to his chair and sat with his crotch scars on blatant display, as if to offer brute corroboration to his story, bottle in one paw, knife in the other.

"My wife, Sonia—Sonia Mendes, she was, before our marriage—was the most beautiful woman I have ever seen. Hair like a waterfall of night, limbs and bosom as ample as a creamery full of butter. When she agreed to marry me, a simple love-smitten gangster—oh, yes, I make no bones about my calling, it is not in my eyes a path more shameful than that of a banker or lawyer—I was completely flattered and grateful, ecstatic beyond words. I could not arrange the wedding fast enough, once I had managed to convince her father of the righteousness of the union. Unfortunately, poor Papa Mendes, who found himself in the hospital shortly after our discussion, was unable to attend the sumptuous affair that united his little Sonia to the humbly born Ovid Reymoa, whose own parents were likewise unable to be present to honor their only son, having been murdered in their sleep years before by certain of my short-sighted business associates with whom I had had a grievous misunderstanding.

"I spent over ten thousand claws that day. The gown Sonia wore—that dress alone cost five hundred scales. We drank and feasted, sang and danced with our guests until early in the morning. Then I took her to our new home—not this mansion yet, but still quite a presentable estate—and fucked her raw in every hole until noon, when I finally allowed her to fall asleep.

"In short, our marriage was off to a fairytale start. Yet the melancholy and perfidy that fills most fairytales was also implicit in our future. For Sonia was not only very beautiful, but very conscious of her beauty. She enjoyed admirers, and, as my business affairs began to involve spending long weeks away from home, she started to acquire a flock of social butterflies who hovered around my gorgeous orchid. Even giving birth to our three children did not dim her luster, nor did she allow motherly duties to interfere with her partying and shopping, her attendance at spas and cotillions. A large staff of servants attended to the upbringing of my three offspring, which might explain their decided lack of respect for their poor old Papa.

"For nearly two decades, I tried my hardest not to be bothered by the busy festive calendar Sonia maintained when I was away, for she was always scrupulous about waiting on me hand and foot whenever I managed to find some time to visit our loving home. No, I was a model, trusting, modern husband, allowing his wife all sorts of liberties commonly reserved to men. It was only when I could no longer deny to myself that those social butterflies had been dipping their long thin spiral tongues into the pollen of my precious flower that I was forced to take action, or suffer the inevitable catcalls of shame from my peers. Despite having considerable proof of her many infidelities, I made no explicit accusations against

Sonia—so much did I still love her—but only forbade her from leaving our mansion in my absence.

"Well, she naturally railed against this prohibition, but after some persuasive arguments, I soon secured her promise to obey.

"As you might have already guessed, her promise was false.

"One day, I arrived home unexpectedly from a trip to Minas Gerais to find Sonia missing from her dutiful post as Senhora Ovid Reymoa, mistress of my holdings and defender of my good name. Thanks to my intimate network of informants, I was soon able to track her down to the lodgings of one Paulo Viera, a slimy boulevardier. With pistol in hand, I went to visit the lovers.

"The outer lock of the apartment yielded noiselessly to my skills, and the bedroom door surrendered to a single kick. Then I had both the naked lovers in my sights.

"At that moment, a flash of fur hurtled across the room at me. I managed to get off a single shot, which flew unerringly into the unfaithful heart of my dear Sonia. Then an enormous mongrel dog—half-wolf, as I later learned—knocked me to the floor and began to savage my genitals, exactly in the manner in which his sadistic owner had trained him to deal with intruders.

"Fighting for my life, I wrestled with the devil-hound, but to no avail. The cruel severing of my balls and mangling of my cock, swiftly followed by an immense loss of blood, rendered me unconscious. I awoke in a hospital, my life saved by the intervention of some neighbors, but with my wife dead—quite legitimately so, in the eyes of the authorities, by the way—and the man who had cuckolded me fled, along with his voracious dog.

"Some months later, I was fit enough to pursue my revenge.

"I traced Viera all the way to Alegrete, a town near the border with Argentina. He had sought to hide by becoming a gaucho, the vocation furthest from his old life. Watching the herds, he and his dog lived alone out on the pampas for long stretches of time. This suited me perfectly.

"One night, employing all my old stalking wiles, after tethering my horse some distance off, I surprised both man and dog sleeping. I dealt with the dog first, shooting him in the hindquarters so as to cripple but not immedi-

ately kill him. Faced with my rifle and my wrath, Viera offered no resistance, instead folding up like a cheap
pocket knife. I roped the man tight, secured the immobilized hybrid dog with a stout noose tossed around its
neck and affixed to a stake hammered into the turf, then
began my wait.

"For the next seven days, I imposed a strict dietary regi-
men on my captives. The dog—his name was, believe it or
not, Bernardo—received only water. Viera enjoyed full
rations, just as I did. That is, at least for the first couple of
days he gratefully accepted his portions, until he de-
duced my plan. Then, after much begging and pleading,
he tried to mount a hunger strike, hoping for a merciful
death by inanition. But I forced food and water into him,
needing him plump and juicy.

"Ah, I will never forget those glorious nights on the
pampas, the stars like a thousand admiring eyes, the low-
ing of the restive beeves, the air so brisk and flavorful. Despite my barely healed crotch, which burned constantly
with a revengeful fire partly real and partly of the mind, I
relished every minute of that time.

"By the seventh day, the skeletal Bernardo was weak
yet ravenously alert. Just out of reach, I offered him my
hand, and he snapped at it without rising. I judged the
moment proper. Bending over, I rolled the screaming
hogtied Viera like a log into the circle of dirt outlined by
the crippled movements of Bernardo.

"The resulting feast was as satisfactory as I had long
imagined it would be. Even though Bernardo dealt with
the soft parts of his master first, the man's agony was sufficiently prolonged to assuage much if not all of my anger.
I continued to monitor Bernardo at his banquet even after
Viera had obviously expired. Then, when the dog had finished, its stomach bulging like a sack full of manioc pudding, I picked up my rifle—

"But I did not use it on the stupefied beast. Instead, I
stashed the gun in the pack that hung from my horse.
When I had my bedroll and other items likewise secured,
I bent to the stake and untied the engorged dog, slipping
the noose from his neck without getting too close. I
mounted up and set off. Breathing heavily, Bernardo
watched me ride away."

Until this moment, the bruja's glimmering eyes had
not wavered from Reymoa's crotch throughout his narra-

115

tive. But now she raised them to his face. Only a mild curiosity layered her self-composed features, and Reymoa fortified himself with another drink against her startling equanimity.

"Why did you not finish your revenge?"

"Bernardo had eaten my balls. My cells were part of him now, all my masculine vigor incorporated into his flesh. Shooting him would have been like shooting myself. He was a brave, brutal, noble creature, only acting as he was taught, and deserved his chance to live free. Considering his wound, his chances were not great. But at least I provided a rich first meal to initiate his new feral career."

"And now that I know your history, how do I figure in this long, unfinished tale?"

Reymoa levered himself out of the chair and approached the bound woman. The alcoholic reek from both captor and captive met and coalesced into a boozy smog.

"I know that you regenerated the arm of Quincas. I just saw your breast rebuild itself. I want you to repair my cock and balls."

"All right. Obviously I will need to be free."

Seemingly taken aback by her easy capitulation, Reymoa paused a moment before saying, "You realize that I will be able to slice your throat instantly, the moment I detect any treachery." He exhibited the machete as if its presence could have been overlooked.

"I hear what you tell me. Do I have your permission to be free?"

After consideration, Reymoa answered, "Very well, let me cut your bonds—"

"That will not be necessary."

Wherever the rope touched the bruja's skin, it begin to smoke and crumble to dry cold ashes, like the pyrotechnic snakes flourished by a stage magician. The naked woman stood up, brushing the cerementous flakes off her unmarked skin.

Reymoa stepped back. "Why—why did you not try to escape earlier?"

Kerry smiled. "But I did not want to escape. I like to meet new people and to help them get whatever they want. Now you, you want to make sweet cum again, loads of it flowing out a big stiff cock. Is that not the case? I can help you."

"What do I have to do?"

"First, take another of my nipples."

Hesitantly, Reymoa approached the woman. She cupped the tit not yet sliced, and smiled invitingly. Alert for any treachery, Reymoa deftly performed a parallel surgery. As before, the bruja's gashed yet unbloodied flesh quickly reengineered its own somatic perfection.

Kerry said, "Give it to me," and Reymoa surrendered the brown corrugated mammary scrap. From the ashtray, the bruja retrieved the first nipple, remarkably fresh and vibrant.

"Now sit down, and open your legs wide."

Reymoa obeyed. "Remember my knife, woman. Since I first honed it at age sixteen, this blade has taken countless lives."

Kerry said nothing, but kneeled before the leather throne, severed nipples rearing like small mountains on the plain of her left palm.

She bent and licked the expanse of scar tissue beneath Reymoa's notched dick. Then she affixed the donated gobs of her own flesh to his crotch where balls should reside. They adhered greedily, incongruous excrescences.

"Your womanly essence—how can this develop into my male parts?"

"I am neither man nor woman, Senhor. I am both and neither. Now be quiet, while I finish this."

Without perceptible transition, the bruja suddenly occupied a kneeling position on the chair's broad arms, so that she straddled Reymoa's lap.

"Now I have to piss on them."

"What? No—" Reymoa attempted to rise, but Kerry's implacable grip upon his shoulders temporarily immobilized him.

A hot forceful urethral jet coined puddles of gold across Reymoa's crotch.

Finished pissing, the woman stood away. Reymoa leapt up.

"No one does that to me and lives!"

"Shut up, you fool. Can you not feel the change?"

Reymoa looked down.

The leech-fast nipples were expanding and swelling, trading one gender-bound configuration for another, wrinkling into a full scrotal sac. Within minutes, Reymoa again possessed a weighty, dangling brace of plummy balls. His expression defined astonishment.

Kerry stepped closer and cupped her handiwork. "Oh, these are fine ones. They will make so much cum, you will not believe it. But first allow me to fix your cock."

With two slippery serum-porous hands, Kerry began to roll Reymoa's mangled cock between her palms as if fashioning a tube of pastry dough. Its substance proliferating exponentially, the truncated member began to fill in missing parts and elongate. All the while, Kerry spoke sweetly and softly into Reymoa's ear.

"Many people are fascinated by the uncrossable border between animate and inanimate. A pebble will never grow into a plant, and a seed will never devolve into diamond. Truly, one of the deep mysteries of existence. But what I find even more intriguing is the distinction between what lives and what once lived. Consider a tree, for instance. Such a marvelous, complex thing while alive. But when chopped down, it becomes mere wood. Yet the wood contains all the elements that once conferred life. What is missing? Where did the life force go? Is it possible to restore it somehow, to some degree? These are the kind of questions that interest me."

Under Kerry's shuffling hands, Reymoa's cock had not only become fully restored, but had lengthened to nearly superhuman dimensions, hanging now a good fifteen inches long, swollen but not rigidly tumescent.

Mesmerized by the regenerative process and by Kerry's whispered philosophical disquisition, Reymoa had said nothing, but now found speech again.

"You may stop now. I do not want to become a monster."

Kerry ceased her manipulations. "I only wanted to make sure you had a cock suitable for the quantity of cum your new balls can produce. Do you feel the swarming animalcules down there? Why, look—I think they are already eager to escape."

Kerry used a green fingernail to retrieve a few silvery pre-orgasmic drops leaking from the slit of the big penis. She held up the exudate for inspection. "The sperm is alive when it leaves you, but soon is dead—unless it finds a hospitable home. Yet what if any once-living substance could afford a welcome as hearty as a woman's womb? This leather, for instance?"

Her fingertip smeared the chair arm, and the cum seemed to seize upon the substance of the chair. Within seconds, a mercury pool shimmered on the chair arm, visibly eating and growing, a badge of resurrection.

"The cum respects what is already alive, of course. Otherwise it would dissolve your very balls. But it fastens eagerly on material that was formerly alive, converting it to its own purposes."

Reymoa grew livid, veins worming his temples. "Madwoman! How can I live this way?"

Homemade blade brutally sliced the air, descending toward Kerry's throat.

Viper-swift, the bruja caught Reymoa's wrist and squeezed until he dropped the machete. She grinned and said, "Oh, you cannot," then drove five fingernails deeply into the nape of his neck to enforce her commands on his spinal impulses. The half-dressed crimelord lost all tonus in his limbs, and Kerry guided his collapse into the chair. On the chair arm the patch of cum burbled and spread.

Silent, yet with lips slightly parted, his eyes remaining open and focused, Reymoa could only watch the bruja's next actions.

"I think we need to establish a good strong flow, just like siphoning water from a hole." Kerry pumped Reymoa's altered dick two-handedly for a minute or so, like a breeder milking a horse. Then, without warning, the cock erupted, not with peristaltically propelled packets of cum, but with a continuous output, a plume of jism. A cohesive column of pungent ejaculate burst outward to splash harmlessly across Kerry's stomach and spangle her bush. Laughing, she closed her eyes and directed the fountain of cum across her face: child with a garden hose. Spunk nectared the back of her throat until she closed her mouth. The ejaculate draped her features, nose, lips and chin, and masked her birthmark. Then she turned the ongoing spray away from herself. Under unvarying muscular pressure, the perpetual orgasmic discharge splattered some four feet away. Wherever it struck wood or leather or paper, it clung and fed. Books became albino amorphous heaps, the floor was decorated with quivering medals of some carnal campaign.

With a free hand, Kerry wiped her eyes clean, and tongued off the lower half of her face with a pink papillary sponge.

"Now we will flush out all your shit, Senhor."

Curving the long semi-flaccid dick around to bring its output to bear on Reymoa's own crotch, Kerry overcame the considerable pressure of the ejaculate to position the glans at Reymoa's asshole. Cum hit the man's sphincter and splashed outward, commencing its assimilation of the chair. Then the woman forced the head of the cock into the ass of its owner, and the ricochet ceased. She fed several inches of the prick deeper into the man, then ran a sealing finger to melt the juncture of cock and hole.

Kerry stepped backward and waited.

Over the dam of Reymoa's lower teeth, past the rampart of his lower lip, pure uncontaminated ejaculate—still hungry despite its hidden fecal intestinal meal—began to spill out, its force diminished by its travels through the man's interior baffles, but the volume of its flow unvarying. The cum riveted his chest, consuming his clothing, meandered across his lap like a skirt, then curtained downward to the floor and began to spread.

Kerry walked away, her partial cum-outlined footprints marking a trail of spreading spermatic ingestion. She let herself out of the library, closing the door behind herself.

On the other side of the barrier, poised in the corridor like Diana in a glade, she heard suggestive sounds: a dissolved chair finally caving in on itself, a body plopping down into a swelling puddle.

Kerry turned toward the rear of the house and padded unerringly to another door.

In their bedroom, Getulio and Hermeto, clad in formal garb suited to the imminent party, were playing cards. Seated at a small baize-topped table, drinks to hand, cigars idling to ashes in silver trays, the brothers turned when Kerry entered. Their eyes widened, but they seemed not overly perturbed by the inexplicable appearance of the naked, semen-soaked woman.

"You must help me," Kerry said. "Your father did this to me."

Hermeto calmly laid his cards face down on the felt and smoothed back his ravenswing of hair. "Ah, dear Papa always did have a fancy for hosting gangfucks. I assume you were hired or abducted to entertain a number of his more influential guests— perhaps some important men advised to arrive early for the tribute to our sister tonight?"

"No. He had me alone."

Getulio smirked. "Papa? I do not see how—"

Kerry strode across the room. "Oh, but does it really matter how? The problem is that all he did was drop his heavy load of spunk on me. He left me very unsatisfied. I have not had a cock up me since I entered this strange house."

Kerry's aromatic unclothed proximity was plainly arousing the men. Getulio said, "Brother, I defer to you."

"But why choose?" Kerry asked. "Two at once would be so much better."

"Have we ever denied anything any lady nicely asked us, Hermeto?"

"Never, little brother. And we certainly have an hour or so to spare before we must witness the coronation of sweet Darciana."

"Oh, wonderful. Then you will both do me right away."

The brothers swiftly disposed of their clothing, careful to lay their swallowtail coats and striped trousers across the bed so as not get them soiled. Kerry dropped to her knees before the naked men and gripped a prick in each hand, an angler proudly displaying two hooked fish. Twin flushed cock heads rested over her thumbs like trophies on a shelf.

She took first Getulio deeply in her mouth. Subtle suctioning noises betokened a unique inward osculation.

"She has a most educated tongue, brother."

"Give her over."

Getulio reluctantly withdrew, and Kerry performed her maneuvers on Hermeto. Both men reached pinnacles of tumescence within a minute.

"Take her cunt from below, little brother. I have a suspicion her asshole will serve my tastes better tonight."

Getulio lay on the rug on his back, and Kerry swiftly straddled him. She reached down to grip his dick for its guided introduction to her cunt. When the recumbent man's cock was fully seated in her vagina, Hermeto squatted behind the pair and brought his prick to Kerry's asshole. The head slipped easily into her anus, and

Hermeto rocked the rest of its veiny length home with a single shove.

For a few seconds, the trio remained motionless and softly groaning. Then Kerry commenced to speak.

"Do you each feel the cock of the other? Such a thin wall separates those two dicks. What if they could touch?"

Hermeto said, "I have just barely filled your asshole, woman. We will both slip up your twat together if you want, but let us have this pleasure first."

"Oh, but I do not mean any such thing. I mean this—"

Getulio's voice contained a trace of nervousness. "Brother, my cock feels as if an octopus has its suckers tightly around the head—"

"Mine too!"

The men attempted to withdraw, but then winced.

"Do not even think of such a thing," Kerry advised. "At least until I allow it. Now, it is time for the two of you to become true brothers."

Down where the pair of cocks pierced Kerry's two mucusy holes, changes were underway. Kerry's perineal area began to flow like cellular lava, drawing her cunt and asshole closer to each other, forcing Hermeto to adjust his awkward stance by dropping his hips. In seconds, the perimeter of her cunt kissed the rim of her asshole, and, like merging bacteria, the two holes fused into one cloaca.

Now it could be seen from the exterior that the two dicks must unavoidably be lying directly against each other inside the monotrematous woman, with Hermeto's balls atop Getulio's like eggs in one nest.

"Brother, I am experiencing the queerest feeling in my cock—"

"I too."

"They are just melting a bit," Kerry said. "There, all finished."

The woman scrambled gracefully out from the human sandwich, a flash of her crotch revealing that her genital area was already restabilizing back to its normal appearance. Deprived of her support, Hermeto scrabbled to adjust his balance, placing his palms on his brother's chest. Then the two men shifted as best they could in order to regard their cocks.

A MOUTHFUL OF TONGUES

Fused completely, underside to underside, the conjoined penises rendered the men Siamese twins of a novel sort.

Kerry stood over the helpless pair. "Scissor your legs together so that you are sitting facing each other. I still want your cum."

Overcome with tears, Getulio only sobbed. Hermeto said, "We would rather perish, you witch!"

Kerry shrugged. "As you command."

The woman reached down and grabbed the men by their double cock. Then, without straining, she dragged the brothers like a human travois out into the hallway. Kerry scraped them along the corridor to the library door, heedless of their protests. At that threshold, Kerry smiled to see a silvery film tentatively seeping under the door.

Kerry swung the door open. A bleachy pungence assaulted their nostrils.

An albescent lake some inches deep, the library was filled with the conquering sperm, which had climbed the shelving to absorb the wood and its unread books (brickwork, resisting, stood revealed); gravity then cooperated in bringing all the absorbed mass down into an homogenous, anonymous spunk pool. The marble top of the library table floated improbably atop the thick sludge. In the center of the jism pond sat Ovid Reymoa, slowly vomiting his own impossibly copious sperm, the altered stuff of his own dwindling organs.

Still half-bent by her grip on the handle of their dicks, Kerry addressed the men. "The cum will not attack your bodies. But you can still drown. I hope this is consistent with your expressed wish to die."

Then she straightened her powerful back, muscles snaking under peachy skin, drawing the men up off the floor by their dicks, so that they dangled backward from the union of their flesh. They yowled as she tossed them into the library.

The pinwheeling splash of their landing was obliterated by the bellow of a close-range shotgun blast.

Two shellsworth of pellets launched from mere feet away lanced across Kerry's left arm, effectively severing it. The partial limb thudded to the floor and began to lurch toward dissolution in the lake of sperm. But already tendrils of flesh hanging from the stump of Kerry's shoulder were writhing, automatically interlacing and capping the protruding bone with a redemptive membrane.

Kerry turned to face her attacker.

Darciana, clad in her tailored party dress, was struggling to reload. She fumbled a shell, brass casing clattering on the floor, and cursed.

"Die, you motherfucking monster, just die!"

Upon the girl in a half a breath, Kerry knocked the gun from her hands. Already, the bruja's lost arm had begun to regenerate: fingertips fruited outward from the sealed butt.

Kerry grabbed Darciana with her undamaged arm and hugged the girl to her naked form. Darciana struggled, but could not escape even this half-hug.

Kerry grinned. "I like you. I like you very much."

From contact with Kerry, Darciana's spectacular dress had begun to melt and drip off her. By the time the girl stood completely naked, Kerry's replacement arm hung fully formed.

The bruja brought her new arm around Darciana, pulling the girl close. Kerry cupped Darciana's ass cheeks and lifted her to her tiptoes. Smaller breasts bobbled larger, thighs pressed thighs, and pubic hair intertwined.

Kerry brought her face an inch away from the girl's.

"Kiss me," she breathily invited.

Then, without detaching her organ, the bruja unrolled twelve inches of her tongue out and down Darciana's throat.

Somehow Darciana continued to breathe, perhaps assisted by her assailant. Thus it was still possible for the girl to gasp when Kerry's cock probed upward and surged past the fairy-wings of the pinioned girl's labia.

A myriad fleshy thorns suddenly pimpled every inch of Kerry's epidermis where she and Darciana touched, a thousand hungry mouths that stabbed into Darciana.

Fluids migrated at hundreds of points from one woman to another, with a curious result.

The women began to swap likenesses.

Kerry lost height, while Darciana grew. Breasts seemed almost to emigrate from one chest to another. Facial cartography experienced the revisionary hand of dictatorial benthic compounds. Limbs took new impressions from those with which they performed this static dance of identity transference.

A MOUTHFUL OF TONGUES

At the end of the process, Kerry/Darciana released her multiple holds on Darciana/Kerry, thorns, cock and tongue withdrawing. The girl wearing the bruja's body staggered backward, eyes cracked wide in utter disbelief.

"I know I will enlarge your reputation, dear," said Kerry. "But are you able to uphold my good name?" The being masquerading as Darciana Reymoa appeared thoughtful. "I do not think so. Into the library with you."

One blow from Kerry rendered her old body unconscious. She picked up Darciana and threw her into the library. The impact of what seemed to be the bruja's shell sent a wave of jism spilling out into the hallway, where it began new conquests.

Kerry skipped lightly away, twirling giddily now and again, as if wearing fifteen once more had filled her with girlish glee.

* * *

A bat chasing insects dipped and flittered like a drunken leaf. A breeze laden with the scent of jasmine and newly cut grass puffed past the spectators at the disaster, then evanesced. Some distance off, a heartbroken dog wailed at the alluringly spurning face of the rising moon.

In the purple light of declining dusk, Arlindo Quincas and Doctor Flávio Zefiro, still as statues, watched in baffled amazement during those first few moments of the rout of the Reymoa household. Only the screams of those being pursued by the unknown coagulated tide and the gritty crunch of the driveway's gravel beneath their feet informed the watchers that they were not inhabiting a dream.

Doctor Zefiro broke the spell by shouting, "Quickly, man! We must help the fallen!"

Quincas broke into a run, bulling past the hurtling servants and heedlessly scrambling earliest guests, and managed to hoist up the teenaged girl who had gone down due to the snare of her own crinolines.

"Are you hurt, Senhorita?"

The girl appeared constrained by shock, and could make no answer. Quincas picked her up and carried her to the nearest carriage, setting her gently down on its plush seats. Then he turned back to the house. Zefiro arrived from his own mercies to stand by Quincas. A third man immediately joined them out of the throng, his stalwart and handsome good looks annotated by a clerical collar.

"Father Texiera, what do you make of this?"

Texiera crossed himself, a scowl causing the knob of his prominent chin to crinkle. "The handiwork of the devil, without a doubt."

The exodus had halted, save for a single woman standing defiantly in the entrance. Dour-faced and militant, incongruously bare-legged beneath her hiked-up black dress, she looked outward toward the assembled gawkers. The riverine flow sluggishly sloshed past this stern Boadicea, shallower than it had looked at first shocking glimpse, only ankle-deep, yet stealthily descending the stairs of the Reymoa house.

"You cowards, come help!" commanded the woman. "This foul stuff is harmless to people! It only eats certain things! We must rescue the master though! I have a suspicion he is hurt!"

Quincas exchanged glances with both Texeira and Flávio, and was rewarded with sympathetic nods of agreement.

"Senhora Soares is right," said Flávio. "We must give whatever aid we can."

"The church has never yet trailed behind the medical establishment in offering succor, Doctor. Let us be about the work of the Lord."

Singling out several of the stunned male servants, Quincas ordered, "You men—get shovels from the toolshed and start digging a trench around the house. We cannot let this strange caustic stuff escape the estate."

The men so nominated rushed to obey, while Quincas, Texeira and Flavio advanced to the slow-moving edge of the flow. After consuming some wooden planters, but not their contents, the sludge seemed at least temporarily stymied by the graveled driveway.

Senhora Soares, lifting her bare foot out of the viscous muck, sought to warn the men of a certain necessary precaution. "It eats clothing and shoes. Dispose of your own shoes, and roll your pants legs up."

The men complied, then entered with repugnance the slow-motion flood. Cautiously they climbed the sloppy, slippery, glycerined steps. Joining Senhora Soares in the doorway, they awaited her orders.

"Senhor Reymoa spent the day in the library. When this crisis struck, I went to look for him there. I arrived at the open library door just in time to witness the floor of the room collapse. Uncertain about the safety of the rest of the second story, I retreated. If we hope to find the Senhor, we must look in the room below the library."

"Lead on, then," said Flávio.

The quartet entered the mansion, with the men wrinkling their noses against the unprecedented assault on their nostrils and flinching at the improprieties committed against their sense of touch. Moving as fast as they could through the redolent slime, they followed the head housekeeper.

"Can this scum be what I imagine it to be, dear Flávio? Does your medical opinion coincide with my obvious guess?"

"I fear so. But of its origins I cannot even speculate."

"I once conducted an exorcism in which copious blood was produced *ex nihilo*, so I imagine Satan would have no problem conjuring up this much semen if he wished."

Senhora Soares's voice was tart. "Quiet, you fools! Lives are at stake, and you debate like a college of pedants!"

They reached the door of the groundfloor lesser ballroom and peered cautiously inside at a lake of ejaculate: the conquering sperm had already swallowed all the room's wooden furniture, setting afloat such items as silver platters, candlesticks, punchbowls and goblets. Then the vision of the rescuers raced upward without impedance to take in the bare walls of the former library on the floor above.

"This place will not stand long if all the interior load-bearing supports are eaten away," ventured Quincas.

"I see four heads of hair!" shouted Senhora Soares. "Quickly!"

Wading deeper into the slime, the lifeguards of this alien pool ineluctably splashed themselves and each other, and their clothing began to melt away. Hurrying, they each latched onto a victim by whatever hold presented itself. Tugging furiously, they dragged the naked bodies out of the ballroom. A crash as of dropping timbers sounded, much too closely, as they cleared the doorway.

"Outside now!"

Abetted by the lubricant of the sludge, the foursome madly hauled their grim cargoes toward the exit, like loggers skidding fallen trees.

"Senhor Quincas," Soares admonished briskly, "your man and mine appear to be joined together somehow. Do not pull so hard!"

Their hasty retreat ended only when the rescuers had stretched out the four obvious corpses upon the lawn. Doctor Zefiro bent over them, cleaning their faces with his monogrammed pocket handkerchief.

"All drowned," came the Doctor's quick diagnosis, followed by a surprisingly heartfelt wail from the normally stony Senhora Soares.

Ovid Reymoa, uro-anally involuted into himself like an empty Klein bottle.

Hermeto and Getulio, melded at the genitals as if in some postpartum womb.

The face of the fourth victim, however, brought only blank stares from the crowd of onlookers expecting to see Darciana. Only one man choked, and cried out in recognition.

"Senhorita Yemana! My dear Jesus, no!"

"You know this woman, Arlindo?"

Quincas could only nod and sob. He bent to pet the jism-filmed cheek of his foreign benefactress and lover.

Attention was drawn away from this tender scene by a loud boom: the roof over the library had fallen inward, as had a good portion of the walls in that wing, sending splashes of ejaculate to soar through the air. Luckily, all the splashes fell within the moated perimeter. Nonetheless, having temporarily desisted from their labors in order to gape at the corpses, the entrenching crew now redoubled their efforts, aided by new volunteers.

"All of our blockade will be for naught," advised Doctor Zefiro, "if anybody leaves here contaminated. We need to dispose of our clothing as well." The doctor regarded his own disintegrating suit with a scientific dispassion, then began to strip.

Quincas made an obvious effort to pull himself together, and managed to sniffle out, "Yes, yes, the safety of the community is paramount."

A MOUTHFUL OF TONGUES

Within a short period, thanks to the organizational skills of the three respected and practical-minded citizens, Quincas, Zefiro and Texeira, as well as the firm hand of a recovered Senhora Soares, a squad of enforcers, inspectors and scrubbers had been formed to round up each witness to the horror and vet them for contamination. Cold water from garden hoses operating on a plumbing system separate from the house's sluiced any quiescent yet deadly cum from bare flesh. Infected clothing was tossed back into the consuming sludge, the terrestrial advance of which had been halted by the trenching. Naked survivors, rinsed clean, huddled temporarily in horse blankets and lap robes until donated clothing from neighbors could be rushed to them.

Dressed in mismatched borrowed apparel, Quincas watched the Reymoa mansion collapse upon itself. Over the course of the next few hours, the trapped devouring colloid assimilated everything organic until all that remained was a stone-walled basement full nearly to overflowing with contaminated ejaculate, a potent stew of roof tiles, bricks, nails, shards of glass, and assorted hardware. Like some kind of industrial vat of molten silver, the foundation full of voracious liquid seemed to await decanting into new molds.

Several fire-fighting apparatuses pulled up now in a creaking of harnesses and clopping of hooves. Doctor Zefiro greeted the professionals.

"Your tanks are filled with those chemicals from the tannery and the paper mill that my messenger specified?"

"Yes, Senhor."

"Start pumping then."

Men began vigorously to work the oscillating pump handles as others aimed the nozzled canvas hoses toward the spermatic pool. The pungent chemicals streamed out to lance the gathered cum. Where they hit, great thrashing boils of steam arose.

Texeira addressed Quincas. "One almost expects screams of demonic frustration to accompany this display."

"Yes, I suppose you might look at it that way."

"What troubles you, my good friend, other than the obvious?"

"The death of that woman. We were close once."

Texeira pondered this statement. "You need my counsel, Arlindo. Please accompany me away from here once we have seen this affair to its conclusion."

"All right, Father."

As gallon after gallon of cell-rupturing chemicals mixed with the lively sperm, the sperm died off, lysing into rancid and vile garbage like putrescent cabbage. Once assured of the pool's irreversible denaturing, Doctor Zefiro ordered, "Spray all the grounds within the moat, men, just to be sure."

Tethered to the scene by his promise to Texeira, Quincas wandered off, circulating among the crowd as if hoping to be alone with his thoughts. Under the deeper mottled darkness of a whispering shade tree, he came upon two women comforting each other. Mutually embracing, one was sobbing, the other silent. Warily, Quincas approached them.

"What ails you, ladies? How can I help?"

A hank of red hair captured a share of moonlight as the crying woman turned her head. "Oh, Senhor, we are doubly sad. Not only did our employers lose their lives, but all the staff have lost their jobs. How shall we survive now?"

Quincas patted the woman's shoulder consolingly. "What is your name, Senhorita?"

"Maura. Maura Colapietro. And this is Mei-mei. She is mute."

"What were your duties?"

Maura smiled. "I was chambermaid to Senhorita Darciana. Mei-mei was her seamstress."

Quincas considered. "I could probably use both of you at my establishment, if your skills as are described. Apply on Monday at The Blue Afternoon."

Maura squealed and threw her arms about Quincas, and, silently but enthusiastically, Mei-mei quickly followed suit.

"How can we ever repay you, Senhor?"

Sweatered in fragrant female flesh, Quincas wore a look of consternation mixed with puzzled delight. "It is nothing, strictly smart business sense to hire talented help." Glancing back toward the destruction, Quincas noted Father Texeira approaching, and he gently unpeeled the grateful pair.

"I must leave you now. Will you be all right?"

"Yes, *now* we will. Who should we ask for at the hotel?"

"Senhor Quincas. Until Monday, then."

Quincas left the happy women and joined Texiera. The priest said, "Let us take your gig, Arlindo, and we will leave mine for the good Doctor. He has already agreed to this plan."

Seated in the moving wagon, the devastated and plague-stricken Reymoa estate falling behind them, the two men remained mostly silent, until Quincas asked, "What time do you have, Father?"

"Nearly ten o'clock PM. Did you have an appointment at this hour?"

"Actually, I did. But I am not sure I possess sufficient spirit now to keep it."

Father Texeira chuckled. "Let me guess. You were intending to visit the house of Senhora Graca to sample her new girls."

"Why, how did you know?"

"Because Ivo invited me also."

"And—and did you accept?"

"Of course. The women from the Three Lakes district are reputed to be incomparable amorists."

"But Father, your vows—"

"Oh, pish and tush on my vows! Vows are kept only in the heart. One may remain bodily chaste, yet be the worst sinner spiritually, while of course the converse is also true. One may sin bodily, yet still be spiritually clean. We are very far away from Rome, my friend, and white men were never meant to live in this licentious tropical climate. After what we just witnessed, can you still assert that life in this lubricious landscape in any way resembles what they deem normal back in Europe? Different climes demand different ethics and different responses, Arlindo."

"I suppose so, Father."

"Please, Arlindo—in light of our mutual destination, call me Baltasar."

"Very well, Fa—Baltasar."

"I assume you will accompany me to our beloved bawdy house on Lemon Street if I assign such a visit as your penance."

"Penance? For what, Fa— I mean, Baltasar, please tell me—what have I done to merit such a strange expiation? I have many crimes of conscience, I admit, like all mortals, but what sin in particular demands that I drown myself in the arms of whores?"

"Your fascination with the dead witch—a fascination close to idolatry."

The reins nearly slipped from Quincas's hands, and he said nothing. Father Texiera allowed his companion to stew a moment, then spoke.

"I know the whole story, Arlindo, straight from the mouths of those porch idlers. And tonight it was an easy leap of deduction to realize that the unknown dead woman back there was your bruja. Undoubtedly, she was responsible for the whole catastrophe we just witnessed. How much better off we are now that she is dead."

Still Quincas remained silent, and Texiera admonished him. "Ah, you cannot find it in your heart to agree with me, can you? That alone is a sure mark of your dangerous obsession with the devil woman. Here is precisely what I mean about being a whited sepulchre, limed on the outside, yet rotten within."

Quincas's voice was forcefully indignant, yet with an undertone of doubt. "Baltasar, if you only knew her as I did—"

"I do not need to. Even if she were the Virgin Herself, your excessive adoration would be dangerous. I can see you do not believe me. Allow me to tell you a story about a colleague of mine. Perhaps you will discern its application to your own life.

"I attended the seminary with Father Joaquim Cabral, and we became good friends, but our first assignments took us on separate paths. Thanks to the grace of God, I ended up in Sao Paulo. Joaquim, however, was sent to Pernambuco, to minister to the cacao farmers. His rural parish had none of the pleasant distractions of the city, none of the urbane company. A sensitive and intelligent, not to mention adequately lusty man, Joaquim was surrounded by barbaric indios and rude farmers, without so much as a single beautiful daughter within miles. And had he laid a finger on any of the indio women, he would have found his shrunken head adorning some chief's belt. The natives of his region were not so tractable as our local aborigines, who have benefited by centuries of proximity to our culture.

"In all too short a time, Joaquim had exhausted his small stock of books, the conversation of the farmers, and

the dry pleasures of onanism. He longed for a female creature on which to spend himself, and even went so far as to
eye the best-groomed, least flea-ridden donkey of the region with barely restrained lust.

"Then he conceived a mad plan.

"It hit him one day that the very product with which
his district abounded could provide him with some so-
lace. I venture to say that he took his inspiration from familiar legends about the crude expedients of ingenious
rubber plantation workers.

"Joaquim commandeered a large batch of cacao pods
from the latest harvest. No one minded, for they were re-
jects deemed inferior for export. With the help of some
native labor, he hulled them and stockpiled enough
beans and other necessary ingredients to make over one
hundred pounds of sweet chocolate. Then he proceeded
to fashion a detailed tin mold in the shape of a woman. He
endowed her with ample ass and breasts, shapely waist
and hips. Between her legs, an inward protrusion of
metal insured the formation of a complementary channel. The pouring hole opened at the crown of her head.

"Came the day of creation, Joaquim and his helpers
slowly filled the lifesized mold with a liquid stream of
chocolate so rich as to be nearly black.

"Joaquim had to guess at the proper cooling period,
and chose to wait several days, keeping the mold im-
mersed in continuously circulating chill river water delivered by an intricate system of flumes. At the end of that
period, trembling with expectation and having dismissed
the indios, he cracked the mold.

"The blank-eyed chocolate woman, save for a small
stem atop her head, was perfect in every detail, down to
the inviting aperture at the juncture of her immobile legs.
And, having been formed precisely to Joaquim's specifi-
cations, she represented his ideal.

"Now, Joaquim imagined he would be able to perform
but a single act of fornication upon the chocolate woman
before the friction of his caresses caused her to melt and
deform. He then imagined that he would render her remains down and recast her, time after time, adding sup-
plementary raw material as necessary to compensate for
any losses.

"But such was not what happened.

"Whether it was due to the supernatural force of his priestly lust or to some diabolism on the part of the indios, the chocolate woman came alive!

"As the naked Joaquim took her up in his arms, she responded passionately. Chocolate eyelids slid upward to reveal chocolate pupils, and a chocolate tongue pushed between her lips and into his mouth. Her legs parted limberly, and her cunt enveloped his stiff member in a tight chocolate vise.

"Joaquim's frustrated instincts took completely over, and he fucked his candy bride like a soldier just back home from battle. After he climaxed up her cunt, he pulled out and his white male elixir drained out of the cul-de-sac of her cunt like filling out of a bitten bonbon.

"The voiceless woman, chocolate to the taste, seemed unharmed by Joaquim's assault, as if her substance were capable of repairing itself instantly—within reasonable limits. It would not be necessary to reconstruct her after each fuck. So now Joaquim had his unique mistress, and was happy.

"But not permanently.

"For months and months, Joaquim enjoyed the pleasures of his cacao-born woman. He took the precaution of having her live in the cool windowless springhouse, where other perishables were stored, so she would not suffer from the heat. But Joaquim did not reckon with drought.

"Invariably, there came a period of intense rainless heat. Under the cloudless skies and blazing sun, first the river shrank and disappeared. Plantations were abandoned, and Joaquim received orders to report back to the bishop for reassignment. But because he knew he could not take his mistress with him, Joaquim disobediently stayed. Then the heretofore reliable spring itself began to falter, its joyful burbling decreasing until at last it ceased completely.

"Unprotected by moisture, the chocolate woman began to melt.

"Joaquim raved and flagellated himself, but to no avail. Within a short time, his woman was nothing but a large fatty mud-colored puddle on the tile floor of his kitchen. Then what do you think Joaquim did, Arlindo? Over the course of the next twenty-four hours, he ate as much of her as he could scrape up, like a savage consuming a ritual sacrifice. Pounds and pounds and pounds of chocolate. He nearly died from it, face smeared, his bowels loosening and his theobromanic heart racing. But he ultimately survived to return to civilization and tell me his sad story, which I now pass on for your edification."

Quincas ventured no comment for some ways down the hill, until he finally asked, "And what finally became of Father Cabral?"

"For his own peace of mind, he had to be sent away from our country, to a land where chocolate is unknown. He ministers at this date to the primitive Patagonians in their frigid Tierra del Fuego. Now, point your nag toward Lemon Street, my friend, and let us celebrate our good luck in having access to an ample supply of conventional flesh."

Number 23-1/2 Lemon Street was a palatial residence fit for an embassy, elaborately corniced and lintelled, its windows all coyly curtained with heavy burgundy drapes. Stone cherubs seemingly borrowed from the entourage of Venus presided over the front door, beside which a discreet brass nameplate proclaimed the madame's name in italic script.

Having parked their buggy at the closest available curbside spot, which was nearly a block away, Quincas and Texiera now stood on the top step before the bordello's door. Slow hooves of a passing tired dray nag conjured rhythmic percussion from Lemon Street's cobbles. As if replying in Morse, Texiera boldly employed the knocker, raising a hard clamor without and within. Quincas shifted nervously from one foot to another.

"Father, I am not certain this is where I should be tonight—"

"Nonsense, man! Ivo and I, as well as your other friends, have discussed your brooding melancholy amongst ourselves and determined that this is precisely the treatment you need. As your pastor, I prescribe this peculiar yet painless penance."

The door swung open noiselessly, revealing a tall busty woman in her late middle years. Clad in a teal satin gown offering a vast expanse of talcumed decolletage, dyed black hair piled high in lacquered roundels, face heavily cosmeticized, she emanated a kind of fossil sexuality, a plump pulchritude.

"Father Baltasar," said the woman with a nervous effusiveness, "how wonderful to greet you tonight. And Senhor Quincas, this is a rare pleasure. Please, enter, enter."

Inside the elegant foyer of the bawdyhouse, door shut, Father Texiera took the madame's hand and planted a kiss thereon.

"Gabriela, you are looking as lavishly attractive as ever."

The flattery glanced off Senhora Graca, her troubled state of mind ever more in evidence. "Thank you, Father. Please, step into the parlor."

The men followed the madame through a tapestry-framed doorway. Falling back behind them, the cloth, printed with Arcadian vignettes, seemed the scrim of some Eleusinian mystery chamber.

Graca's carpeted parlor contained a half-dozen velvet couches and a grand piano, as well as much Laocoonian erotic statuary and a small bar well-stocked with the more popular brands. But the piano bench held no player and absent also was the bartender. To the contrary, every square inch of seating, as well as the scrollwork arms of the couches, hosted idle resting whores. Gaslights in amber globes caramelized their assorted skin tones, and in their studied provocative opulence the women resembled a flock of heterogeneous birds of paradise, a score of cousin species gathered around some waterhole; or, less wholesomely, assorted competitive carrion feeders collected around a corpse.

The women launched an arrow-sharp fusillade of bright smiles and seductive glances at the two newcomers. Father Texiera's gaze appreciatively took in the sultanate's worth of womanly skin, before he turned with a puzzled expression to Senhora Graca.

"But Gabriela, this crowd appears to consist of every girl in your house, including the newest. Who is entertaining the patrons? From the difficulty we had finding a spot to tether our horse, I would have guessed you had no fewer than fifty customers. And where is the talented Amerigo, whose fingers graze the ivory keyboard like little lambs? And what of your wizardly Magali, who can turn the simplest ingredients into ambrosia?"

Graca began to sniffle, and the assembled whores grew grim, frightened or spiteful looking.

"Oh, Father, everything has gone askew! After tonight I am sure to be ruined! And it is all the fault of that dreadful Reymoa tart!"

"Darciana?" asked Quincas, fingers raking his mustache in puzzlement. "But surely she too must have died in the collapse of the mansion. Or so all of us assumed!"

Senhora Graca's worry transformed to irritation. "Collapse of the mansion? What are you babbling about, Quincas? It is as obvious as the nipple on my left tit what happened. The girl cracked under the responsibility of her coming-out party, and fled. She showed up here on my doorstep some hours ago, as imperial as any princess, and demanded to be let inside and established in my largest bedroom. Since then, she has been fucking every man who has stepped across my threshold, not excluding my own employees, monopolizing them all and denying both me and my girls our proper income for the night!"

"This is impossible! Perhaps the girl was driven mad by the chaos at the estate, and then managed to escape—"

"Chaos? Again, what chaos?"

"You really haven't heard? Tell her, Father."

Texiera described the uncanny recent fall of the house of Reymoa, Senhora Graca and the whores hanging on his every word as if by their fingertips to a precipice. When he had finished his story, Senhora Graca exhibited even more confusion and unease than prior.

"I do not know what to make of any of this. But at least if that horrid tyrant Ovid Reymoa is truly dead, then perhaps the political repercussions of tonight will be lessened for me. I suppose you two may as well go up and join the rest of the rutting boars. Perhaps you can convey the fate of her family to Darciana, despite her nymphomaniacal frenzy. If not, then, judging from what I've witnessed so far, at least you'll have one hell of a fuck."

The long curving staircase rising to the second floor seemed to stretch forever, an endless frozen waterfall of marble steps. Texiera and Quincas ascended without speaking. Nervous sweat stippled the latter's brow. At the head of the stairs, Texiera paused to remove and pocket his clerical collar. Then the two men moved down the corridor toward an open door from which wavering candlelight and a gabble of noise escaped.

Elaborately canopied, the four-poster bed could barely be discerned for the crush of naked men surrounding it:

shoulders broad or slumping, chests slabbed or flabby, guts taut or sagging, hairy asses plump or sculpted, spindle shanks or athletic calves. Nearly three-score men crowded the room, filling it with a hormonal reek. Exhibiting a catalog of techniques, the men assiduously worked their own overwrought pricks in anticipation of a chance at the prize obscured but immanent on the bed: with two hands or one, fingers curling their tubes of meat ventrally or dorsally, lingering on shaft or head, cupping balls or resting a relay hand on a cocked hip, the masturbators sought to keep themselves just at the peak of their lusts without spilling seed. If they made any sound at all, they grunted or offered single-word exhortations.

Unnoticed as yet, Quincas and Father Texiera regarded the orgy from the doorway for a moment. Then the priest began to unbutton his shirt. Quincas looked on with alarm.

"Surely you do not propose to take part in this shameless bacchanalia, Baltasar?"

"When will I ever have such an opportunity again, Arlindo? I see here only a semblance of the love-feasts of the earliest communal Christians."

"I would not know about such things, Father—"

Baltasar was soon naked, and pushing forward into the crowd. Quincas, still stubbornly clothed, nonetheless followed him instinctively.

"The priest, the priest!" "Make way for the good Father!" "Let him officiate at this youngster's confirmation!"

The newcomers broke through the ring of men.

Utterly exposed, Darciana Reymoa lay on her back across the width of the bed, her head hanging partly off one edge of the mattress so that her long hair brushed the floor. Her lithe girlish body, maculated with enough recent cum explosions to make it seem almost as if she had not truly escaped the mansion unmarked, now satisfied five men.

By coincidence or arrangement, the quintet of fucking men was synonymous with the party of idlers who ruled the porch of The Blue Afternoon.

Between Darciana's yawning legs, the ponderous huffing Ivo plumbed her cunt, his thickish cock stretching her rubescent hole wide.

A MOUTHFUL OF TONGUES

Kneeling on the bed so as to bracket her breasts, dimpling the coverlet, the nominal head of the group, Ricardo, and its youngest member, Belmiro, enjoyed Darciana's firm manual sliding grip on their respective cocks, one senescently semi-flaccid, the other stallion-tumescent. From the latter, Belmiro's, a long drip of clear lubricant spidered down to web Darciana's nipple.

Standing by her head, the cadaverous Estevao and the fidgety Januario fed substantial portions of their own dicks simultaneously past her stretched lips and into her concaved cheeks, two crossing lances goring a she-dragon.

Sidling up behind Ivo, Father Texiera pondered the energetic actors with an anticipatory gleam in his eyes. As if hypnotized, Quincas likewise watched.

Ivo came first, rocking Darciana's pelvis with his final impulsive thrusts backed by his excess poundage. Then both mouth-milked cocks surrendered their gulleted essences. Belmiro launched a plethora of spunk entirely across Darciana's body to splatter Ricardo's belly. As if a trigger, that hot burst set off the older man's lesser pseudolactic dappling across one of Darciana's tits.

The five men relinquished their spots, already stroking themselves up for another round, and Darciana wiggled upright to a sitting position, unvanquished and insatiable.

"Oh, our favorite priest." Her slickened smile beckoned. "You are just the man I have been awaiting. Will you have my ass?"

She flipped over onto all fours, presenting her shiny rump.

Texiera stepped forward, engorged cock in hand. He brought glans to anus, grabbed her hips and pulled her onto himself, sleeving his dick in one motion.

Darciana cooed, then looked backward, chin nudging her left shoulder.

"Kiss me, Father."

The tip of her tongue pinked the air.

Texiera bent forward and brought his mouth close to hers.

Almost subliminally, across the narrow gap shot the sensate unmoored organ.

Texiera gulped, then swallowed.

Only Quincas seemed to observe this anatomical impossibility. He shied back a step, but halted when Darciana winked at him and flicked what was apparently the same tongue still safely housed in her mouth.

Almost immediately, as if responding to a puppeteer's string-pulling, a blank-eyed Texiera commenced to pound Darciana's ass.

"Everyone, kiss me now! Do as I say, you rotten cocks! Kiss me!"

Apparently unwilling to displease the object of their lusts, the cunt-smitten men obeyed. Lining up in orderly fashion, one by one, they bussed the dirty, depthless mouthful of tongues.

After many replenished kisses, something began to happen to Texiera. Quincas watched in astonishment.

The priest had ceased fucking without climaxing first, and had collapsed atop Darciana's supportive back. The interface between them was hazy. A blast of heat suddenly radiated off the conjoined bodies, and Texiera seemed to sag and partially melt into the woman.

With superhuman strength and agility, Darciana hurled both herself and the priest through one hundred and eighty degrees of rotation so that the male landed below her against the mattress. But only an increasingly flattening remnant of Texiera remained, as his absorption accelerated, his limbs sinking into hers, his face invading the back of her skull. And every ounce of the priest's diminishing mass went to increase Darciana's bulk, gravitating in perfect ratios to every spot of her amazing body.

In such a short time for so drastic an amalgam, an Amazonian-proportioned Darciana lay alone on the bed.

"Next!" she cried. "Who will be next!"

Will-less, the tongue-invaded males drew in upon her as if falling down a well.

The subsequent absorptions were hardly as decorous as the first. Scrambling, lurching, clambering over each other, the men sought to press themselves against Darciana. What resulted was a maelstrom of flesh, a tangled congeries of parts. Legs and arms stuck up at odd angles from a living quivering boulder of flesh, and headless torsos disappeared into the squirming pile. No male element escaped ingestion for long, however, and from minute to minute a confused image of the ever-swelling

Darciana would emerge, her face ecstatic, until the next infalling victim obscured her outlines.

The orgy continued to collapse exponentially into a singularity as Quincas backed slowly away, abject horror written luridly across his features.

With a splintery crash the bed collapsed under the weight of the gargantuan woman. Within mere minutes, feeding off her hapless suitors, she extended from one side of the room to the other. Still men hurled themselves into her as if into the sea, each one succumbing more quickly than the one before, as their bodies contributed less percentagewise to the vortex of her omnivorous totipotency.

Quincas stumbled at the threshold of the room. When he recovered himself and looked back, the supine giantess no longer wore the likeness of Darciana Reymoa.

A facial birthmark big as a vat of claret seemed to pulse to the pounding of a whale's heart socketed beneath tits vast as prize-winning wheels of cheese.

"Senhorita Yemana—"

The titaness extended arms big as a bundle of telegraph poles toward him, knocking over the candle-topped bureau.

"Arlindo!" Her voice blew the panes of the windows outward, the reciprocal inward gust of her inhalation fanning a young conflagration midst the curtains, and the roaring of his name made Quincas scream.

"As you desired me, so you find me! Come to me now!"

Holding his bleeding ears, Quincas turned and ran.

He missed the final stair and tumbled, his chin scuffing the marble. When he found his feet, he was nearly knocked over again by a torrent of screaming whores, a perfumed avalanche of lace and high heels.

"Fire! Fire!"

Somehow he was out on the street, looking back at the flame-quickened upper stories of the bordello.

A hand dropped onto his shoulder.

Quincas turned to confront the stoic visage of Ixay, his indio gardener. Yeena the barmaid stood beside him, and behind those two waited at least another dozen Dartpipe aborigines.

Ixay's voice was calm, his face placid. "Go home, Senhor. The night is old, and we are in charge now."

* * *

A banausic sun hammered golden spikes of light into the jade roof of the jungle. Inexhaustible gallons of water vegetatively respired to aerosols blanketed the land with humidity. Butterflies erratically mapped invisible roads among the flowered boughs, while immense dragonflies slatted and unslatted their gemmed wings down more direct aerial trails. Armored like the chargers of miniature knights, lizards jousted. Parrots chattered, monkeys capered, and nocturnal creatures slept, uneasy limbic visions rising and fading in their small minds.

Down a rutted, center-humped dirt road, a meager channel through the sprawling jungle held at bay only by regular machete assaults—as evidenced by the route's recently hacked borders, where stripped branches bled sap—a majestic flat-bedded, stake-sided wagon intended for hauling huge logs, entire felled arboreal giants, trundled along under the impetus of ten straining horses gee'd onward by a lone seated native driver, who removed his straw hat from time to time to bat at hovering flies. Pacing the slow carriage on foot were a handful of Dartpipe men and women, among them Ixay and Yeena. These two former servants still wore the clothing of the whites, as did some of their companions; but most of the walkers maintained a more traditional dress: naked scribed chests on both men and women, a profusion of beads and of bone ornaments, painted decorative cartouches across cheek and brow, loins aired by flap coverings.

The contents of the wagon bulked huge but concealed, an enormous old tattered sail from a clipper ship draped across some long irregular rotundity and secured by many lashings. The material of the sail was consistently darkened as if recently splashed with barrels of water, although certain splotches here and there showed a darker hue, as if due to a more complex seepage from underneath.

Striding along untiringly back near a rear wheel, accompanied by a cicada castaneting of her vaginal rings, Yeena touched an edge of the canvas. "Do you think the covering will stay damp for the rest of the journey, Ixay?"

"I believe so. We have no way to refresh the protection in any case until we reach the village."

A MOUTHFUL OF TONGUES

Yeena regarded the foothilled landscape of the canvas for a time, as if searching for some sign of the state of the hidden cargo. "Do you think the saint is still alive? The damage was severe."

"More than the purest flame is needed to end the life of one such. I do not worry about the survival of the saint. I worry about the survival of the tribe."

"What do you mean?"

"I suspect that Xexeo will see only a single path for us to take, in order to manage the presence of the mad saint, and that path leads but one way, into a strange territory from which there is no return."

Yeena reached for Ixay's hand and held it. "I am not afraid of death if I can greet it with two lovers such as you and Tulikawa, Ixay."

Ixay smiled grimly. "Who spoke of such a simple thing as death, little beetle?"

Like a slow-witted pilgrim who never reached his ultimate destination no matter how many months and years he traveled, the sun traced its familiar arc across the lazuline sky. Little conversation obtruded among the indios and indias as they plodded along without halting for meal or refreshment, taking their leaf-wrapped victuals and gourd-bottled drink on the move.

The road began to slope upward, and the horses were forced to greater exertions. Midway up a long grade, the humans gathered behind the wagon to add their strength to the task. Muscles bunched in back and thigh, sweat popped out across pastures of exposed bronze skin like flowers after a desert rainfall, and breath rasped.

A massive rock, striated with the record of its geologically catastrophic bad luck, part of some larger ledge perhaps, reared its head in one rut, frustrating progress. The people gathered on that side of the wagon and labored mightily. Eventually the wagon surmounted the aggressive rock, dropping heavily back down on the far side. The jolt bounced the wagon and its load, and something shifted.

From beneath a gap at the bottom of the canvas, part of a finger the size of a one-person canoe protruded. The pink meat of the digit was partially cooked, skin blackened and split. The scarab-green fingernail, wide as platter for serving a whole roast suckling, hung on to its substrate precariously.

143

The Dartpipes attempted to return the finger to the protection of the covering, but were unable to adjust the massive hand it belonged to sufficiently without undoing the canvas.

"Let it be," advised Ixay. "We will arrive home soon."

Another forty-five minutes brought the wagon to an overlook: threaded by the descending road, the quilt of the jungle dropped away to a littoral plain and the boundless, bountiful sea. Planted close to the water was the Dartpipe village, its beautiful symmetry suggesting a mandala.

The tang of salt air and the sight of their homes delivered fresh energy to the travelers, and they prepared for the descent, each wheel requiring four hands to pull on the lever of a crude brake as directed by the driver.

Carefully, with murmured prayers and curses, the people and wagon descended the long slope toward the sea, losing sight of their destination as they entered the chute of foliage. The humidity dispersed with every foot they descended, and in a short time, without further incident, the cortege arrived on level ground, where the jungle trailed off into saline marshes and water meadows ripe with waving cattails and seagrasses, with splashing fish and stalking, long-legged birds. Here the road resembled more a twisting dike whose narrow top forced the walkers to trail the wagon. Making all possible speed, the procession soon reached the village, whose low acreage represented the largest expanse of dry land in sight.

Concentric on the largest long hut—whose thatched roof stretched some thirty feet above plaited walls—the village grew outward in rings of lesser dwellings, all trim and well-maintained, separated from their ringmates by irregular spacings and linked by narrow meandering paths paved with finely crushed shells. The shells sparkled, mostly white but with a fair percentage of rose, periwinkle and coral tones. On the opposite side of the village from where the road pierced the invisible palisade, a broad sandy avenue led toward the sea, roughly half a mile distant.

Yeena wrinkled her nose appreciatively as the wagon's driver halted the procession on the village outskirts. "I smell monkey cooking. And tapir."

"Chief Paiwe has undoubtedly laid on a feast. Only after we are all well fed and full of maté, only after all the old songs have been sung one last time, only then will the discussion about the mad saint take place, led by Xexeo. This is as it should be, of course. Who can make an intelligent decision without honoring the old ways first?"

Ixay and Yeena, along with the other returning Dartpipes, stepped gratefully away from the wagon and its taut-tarp'd cargo to be welcomed home by the rapidly assembling villagers, gracile men, milk-breasted women, nubile maidens and fat-cheeked children. In the midst of this excited crowd, the handsome head and torso of one young man was elevated as he appeared to be upborne by a hidden horse whose long swishing tail gently swatted the villagers who rested against the horse's flanks.

Spotting the riding youth, Yeena called out, "Tulikawa!" The man waved in reply, but could not come closer due to the press of people.

At the head of the committee stood two radically dissimilar men. The first, perhaps some fifty years old, wore a long European-style striped cotton nightshirt over pronounced potbelly and plump legs. The sleeves of the garment had been ripped off and discarded, to reveal biceps that sagged like the belly of a pregnant cat. Cheerful and beaming, the gowned man had completed his outfit with the addition of a misknotted silk cravat.

Standing next to this cheerful leader was a shamanistic figure. Incredibly aged yet somehow ageless, naked save for a penis sheath pinned by a sharp needle of bone through his foreskin, the second man was festooned with feathers and bone ornaments. His skin was traced with a painted labyrinth, prominent ribs and wiry limbs representing a maze with no ingress or egress, and his face a whirlpool of color. Straw matted with pigmented muds formed a kind of crown sitting high above his pendulous ears. An enigmatically stuffed and heavy leather poke hung from a leather string around his narrow waist. Clutching a notched and fetish-adorned staff, the top of which boasted the secured skull of a large cat, a jaguar perhaps, the man seemed some weedy plant rooted next to its trellis.

Ixay stepped forward and embraced the plump nightshirted man. "Chief Paiwe, we have returned safely with the mad saint, as our shaman dictated."

Ixay nodded humbly at the naked elder standing next to the headman. Xexeo only stared back with cold assessment.

Chief Paiwe clapped Ixay heartily on the back. His voice seemed to rumble out of a cask. "Well done! Your name will long be honored."

Xexeo lowered his staff to allow the bleached skull to graze Ixay's shoulder, and the former gardener jumped galvanically. When Xexeo spoke, it was as if a cloud had gone over the sun.

"Almost I could wish you had failed. This moment marks the end of our life as we have known it."

Chief Paiwe tried to bluster past this doomful pronouncement. "Much remains to be seen. But one thing I know. The sun is dropping and the clams steaming in their shells are crying out to be swallowed! Let us go now to the longhouse and enjoy the bounty of the land and sea!"

Xexeo raised his staff. "Wait! The saint needs to be watered. Soak the covering, but make sure to use only fresh water. Let not so much as a drop of seawater touch that shroud!"

Chief Paiwe repeated the order, but his imprimatur was obviously superfluous, since a group of the shaman's acolytes were already scurrying to obey.

The majority of the villagers swarmed toward the promised banquet. Eventually, only the shaman Xexeo remained behind.

Water dripped slowly from the titaness's exposed fingertip, tinted the lightest pink. Xexeo cupped a hand beneath the spill, and when he had accumulated a small pool in his palm, consumed the liquid with a delicate pointed tongue, smacked his lips, nodded sagely, then moved off to join his flock.

Night had descended fully, risen clipped moon Odinically ocular, by the time the banquet got fully underway. The walls of the longhouse seemed to balloon with the aromatic smoke from both torches and cooking fires, and the interior of the hut pulsed with noisy energy. Palm leaf platters hosted roasted meats, fat shrimps, poached fish, tubs of vegetables, mashed and whole, bowls of grainy puddings, and tuns of maté. Individual shell dishes and coconut cups, filled to capacity and beyond, rested in the laps of the feasters. Chief Paiwe,

A MOUTHFUL OF TONGUES

Xexeo and Ixay occupied a central divan of fronds. The Chief upheld a trencherman's reputation, Xexeo chewed a single mouthful of some unmasticatable root, and Ixay moderately replenished his trek-fatigued body.

Right at the open door of the longhouse, Yeena sat next to Tulikawa, her arms around his waist, children falling all over the happy couple. A blanket covered the legs of the lovers against the maritime evening breezes.

After hours of eating, drinking and singing, laughter and boasts, Chief Paiwe stood up with no small effort and motioned for silence.

"Our shaman will speak now, and advise us about the saint."

With the aid of his staff, Xexeo nimbly found his feet. Facing his attentive audience, he kept them waiting for long seconds before uttering his first words.

"A mad saint has come among us, and we are both blessed and cursed. Blessed, for the arrival of the saint signals that our people have been selected to transcend to another level of existence. And cursed, for such a nomination means leaving behind all the familiar comforts and sorrows that have occupied us until now."

Ixay interjected a question into a pause. "Can we deny this simultaneous honor and burden, Shaman? Turn our backs on the saint and go on with our simple lives?"

"No. And I will tell you why. The saint is unkillable. Soon she will recover from her hurts, emerge from her coma with our help or without. Then, because she is mad, because she is foreign-born and not trained in the true path, she will continue to wreak havoc in Bahia and beyond, her powers ungoverned by any real wisdom. To remain true to our ancestors, we must assume the responsibility for her chastisement and education. And the only way to do so is to join her on her own plane of reality."

Chief Paiwe wore a frown as if trying on the expression for the first time in his life. "When would we go to join the saint?"

"There is no point in putting off our inevitable destiny. We should welcome it gladly, as we would welcome a prodigal child. One more week—one more month, one more year—of mortal life will not add more than a stick to our bonfire of knowledge and memories. Let us take this grim and needful plunge directly upon the morrow."

A shocked communal sound as of a woman in child-birth or a warrior in battle sprang from the villagers. Several of the youngest children began to cry. Chief Paiwe asked a final question.

"Can we be certain the gods approve of this action? Are we not perhaps being overproud in deciding we are worthy to emulate the saint?"

Xexeo smiled confidently. "I have come prepared to ask the approval of the gods. We will plant the Dry Toad now."

The fronded couch was quickly disassembled by eager acolytes, revealing a patch of bare earth. With the sharpened end of his staff, Xexeo chipped a hole big as two fists in the packed earth. Then he undid the poke from his belt, slipped its lacing, and upended it over the hole.

From the leather sack tumbled a living toad, landing upright with a succulent plop. The toad did not try to escape the hole, but remained in place for the ritual.

An acolyte brought Xexeo a scuttle full of hot coals.

"Open your mouth, celestial messenger."

The toad obeyed, pouched maw gaping, and Xexeo funnelled the embers down its throat. The toad did not flinch, but calmly swallowed the radiant charcoal.

"I bury you under a foot of earth," chanted the shaman. "I put you under my feet. Deliver my prayers to the gods, Dry Toad, and bring me their answer swift. The waves of the sea be my deliverance, peace come to me in the dust of the earth."

Bare calloused soles scuffled dirt over the unblinking sacrificial amphibian. Xexeo turned back to the crowd.

"We will have our sign in the morning. But since I do not expect the gods to deny our course, I would advise all of you to regard this night as your last in mortal form."

Under this somber injunction, the sated and pensive feasters dispersed.

A pocked jester, the moon shed its laughter as sardonic light across the village, guiding the steps of the Dartpipes back to their huts. Surf boomed on the nearby strand. Halfway across the village, Ixay, trudging contemplatively alone, received without warning the clutch of a small hand on his shoulder, bringing him to a halt.

"Yeena. I thought you would be with Tulikawa."

Upturned, filmed with lunar glory, the former barmaid's pretty face wore an untroubled grin. "He waits for me at his stable. I told him I would meet him some hours after midnight. But right now I wish for us to be together."

"I too. But I did not dare ask."

"Foolish man! I hope I do not have to take charge with everything!"

Ixay pinched her thigh and replied, "No, I see some courses of action quite clearly."

They gripped hands and headed off. Sounds of amorous foreplay began to drift through the night air, rendering the pair quietly reflective, until Ixay spoke.

"Do you think I have doomed our people, Yeena, by bringing the saint here? When I first saw her, I thought she was only a bruja, and of no great consequence. But she turned out to be so much more . . . "

"Worrisome man! We did the only responsible thing. Only our kind can tame this one. Besides, is our destiny not a glorious one?"

"Glorious? I suppose. But will we be in any condition to appreciate it?"

"Maybe. Maybe not. So we enjoy ourselves right now."

The inside of the sparely furnished hut the lovers eventually entered was lit only by a lambent wick floating in a shallow cup of palmnut oil. Its desultory glow rendered Yeena's naked form into a canvas of shadow and gold, tattooed breasts, bush and buttocks, and gilded Ixay's bare musculature with medieval parchment garnish.

Yeena kneeled before a standing Ixay and pushed his stiffening prick up and back to rest against his stomach. Revealed was a genital piercing: a short wooden peg ran through the upper looseness of his scrotal sac just at the base of his cock, exiting on either side.

Not neglecting to wash the old gnarly scars where the peg protruded, Yeena tongued Ixay's balls and the root of his cock. Then her lips wetly enveloped his prick, sliding rootward nearly to the peg. Ixay cradled her chin and let her bobbingly throat him for a minute. Then he pushed her gently onto her back and climbed between her angled legs. Guiding his dick into her tender ornamented cunt, he buried himself up to his piercing and hers, then paused.

Yeena reached down with both hands to snag her labial rings. Expertly, she slipped one over each end of Ixay's stubby hitching post.

Linked by their pudendal jewelry, the pair began to fuck. Ixay's strokes were necessarily shortened, for at the apogee of each withdrawal, Yeena's inner cunt lips and his loose scrotal wrinkles were stretched to their limits. But the tension and release of the pulling, along with the heightened concentration necessary not to cause hurt, seemed to fuel their fucking with extraordinary potency. When Yeena began passionately to cry out, Ixay too released a torrent of wordless exclamations, and soon they reached a mutual enchained climax.

Falling atop Yeena, Ixay rolled them over onto their sides. Still linked, Ixay shortly fell asleep. Yeena watched over him until slumber had fully claimed the man. Unhitching herself, she left the hut still naked.

The villagers continued to fill the night with sounds of a final human ardency as Yeena stepped quickly across the settlement. She dipped a hand into her snatch and cupped one breast in empathetic response.

From outside his spacious living quarters, through a waist-high window, the painted face and chest of Tulikawa could be glimpsed, as he sewed at a length of fabric: his needle and thread dipped and flew like a hummingbird trailing brightness. Yeena stepped inside, and when Tulikawa saw her his look of intense concentration fragmented into joy. He set his sewing down on a narrow table and got to his feet.

Four horny hooves bladed the chopped earth of his pungent stable home. His excited tail swiped a mug off a high shelf to shatter. Smiling at Yeena, Tulikawa absentmindedly scratched the transition zone of his midriff where skin segued by degrees to chestnut horsehide.

"It seemed you would never arrive! Look, I have been working on this garment ever since your last visit home! It is finished now—I was just fussing with it." The centaur held up his handiwork: a shawl picked out with floral embroidery. "I intend it for you, of course."

Yeena accepted the gift, a tear hanging in the corner of one eye. "So beautiful. Thank you, Tuli. Look, I will wear it from now until the end." She draped the shawl about her shoulders, then stepped forward to hug the centaur. The disparity in their heights allowed her only to embrace his human midsection.

"Oh, no," said Tulikawa humorously. "So many hours of work surely merit more than a hug!"

A MOUTHFUL OF TONGUES

Yeena grinned back at the hybrid. "A kiss, then. I will stand on the chair your visitors use." She climbed atop the seat, and Tulikawa clopped forward. Now their heads were on a level, and they began to kiss with fervor, Yeena's calligraphied breasts nuzzling the centaur's chest. After some time Tulikawa reached a hand down to play with Yeena's moist cunt. She thrust against his exploratory fingers, grinding as much of herself against him from neck downward as she could.

They broke apart, and Yeena sighed. "Oh, Tuli, how I wish we could go on kissing while we fuck!"

Tuli tried to look sad, but failed. "My body is misshapen from the mortal norm, Yeena. But it offers other considerations you have been known to call adequate compensation."

Yeena stepped off the chair and dropped an arm over Tulikawa's withers. "Let us see just how your compensation is doing." Still holding on, she bent forward to bring her eyes level with the equine belly.

A livid cock, measurable in feet and thick as a mangrove root, bounced with its own blood-eagerness. From its spatulate velvet head already drooled copious ropes of pre-cum.

All in a practiced flash, Yeena released the centaur and he jogged his forehooves up onto the chair, making it easier for her to slip underneath him and assume a comfortable squatting position.

Yeena rubbed first one cheek, then the other against the horsecock, snailing liquid across her face. Extending her arms straight out and back, she encased the long dick between her forearms, her fingertips just tickling the loose horsey balls, trapping the rigid flesh in a soft vise. She brought her mouth to the swollen head, and managed merely to cap it. She began a sensuous frottage of the horsecock, maintaining her mouth in place to capture all the early juices, until Tulikawa's hindquarters began involuntarily to buck for more.

Yeena emerged from beneath the centaur, who dropped down off the chair. She moved to the narrow table and spread the shawl across it, then boosted herself upon the top. On her back, she motioned the centaur to cover her. Tulikawa eagerly pranced forward to roof her.

Yeena's cunt needed only a slight assistance from her braced feet to elevate the few inches that separated it from the bobbing horsecock. She reached down to grasp the tiller of this furred ship and socket it against the canny steerswoman of her cunt.

Canopying the woman, Tulikawa stepped forward, and Yeena gasped. Like a rod of dark heartwood cored from some exotic tree, his prick split her cunt like a ripe fruit, forcing her stone ornaments outward into the flesh of her crotch. She hurled her arms backwards to clutch the table edge. She dropped her legs to curl them around the table supports. Fixed in place, anchored by the solid furniture, she invited the massive organ deeper within.

Inch by inch Tulikawa doweled his cock into the blissfully crucified woman, flexing her vaginal aperture into wider and wider liberty, until she had taken well over thirteen thick fat inches inside her. The centaur's sigil-decorated human face reflected his appreciation of the exquisite union. Slowly, now that his cock had measured her depth, he began to fuck her.

Yeena's ecstatic screams split the night. The table rocked like a skiff in a gale, but held.

When Tulikawa finally released his bounteous jism, the cargo overflowed even her massively plugged twat, puddling the table. He pulled out, and with that undamming the rest of the rich roux flooded out like a spumey freshet, soaking the shawl.

Tulikawa stepped away, uncovering the woman. Yeena remained unmoving upon the table, eyelids lowered, limbs lax, until he trotted around to her head, bent at his human waist and kissed her brow. Paired lashes separated, and she raised a hand to pet his face.

"Did we mar your delicate stitchery? No matter, I will still wear the shawl as I promised, the scent of your spunk close to my breath when we go to face our fate."

"At least we go together as a tribe. If two such as we, who have been friends since childhood, had to face our end alone, I would be sad. But having you and Ixay and all the others in my sight tomorrow will bring only happiness."

"So say I, Tuli—so say I too."

The natural catalogue of the morning's delights varied not at all on this special day. Gentle breezes heralded the sun's brave ascent. Like divas, the clouds gave way in gaudy exits from the stage of the sky. Wakening wildlife called out, as did domestic animals, the first class rudely, the second with the polite grace that derived from regular feedings. The latter clan were met this fateful morning, however, not with pails and knives, but with freedom: uncooped, uncorraled, unleashed, and shooed off to fend for themselves. Another anomaly: no odors of cooking rose from the family hearths, no sounds of washing or hunt-preparation obtained. Instead, one by one the villagers emerged from their huts, bleary-eyed and disheveled, to gravitate toward the longhouse.

Xexeo already awaited them, his old-man's chest puffed out with pride at the manifestation of the gods' blessing, his skull-topped scepter grinning along with him.

Through the roof of the longhouse a tree had shot up overnight. Fully leafed, with exactly three individually proportioned branches, red, white and black, the tree born out of the Dry Toad rustled suggestively in the wind, as if whispering secrets from another dimension.

Xexeo brought the crowd under the umbrella of his confident voice.

"The signs are clear! You know that the white branch is always love, the red despair, and the black mourning. But note the ratios! Love is largest, despair moderate, and mourning smallest. Today we must go to meet our destiny!"

A voice called from the fringes of the crowd. "Am I late? Can I still join in? Let me through!"

A young mestizo man in city garb wedged himself though the crowd to confront the shaman.

"Who are you? Why do you disturb us at this sacred time?"

"Xexeo, it is I, Caozinho!"

"Caozinho?"

"Once Caozinha, daughter of Zetwara and the white man, Lazaro Sabino."

The crowd laughed, until silenced by the shaman.

"You bear some resemblance to the daughter of Zetwara, but you are plainly not a woman now. How can this be?"

Caozinho gestured toward where the recumbent mass still bulked out the tarp-covered wagon. "I had an encounter with your saint. She swapped the sexes of my father and myself. Afterwards, we moved to the town, where my father—my new mother—took up a fresh career as a whore at the house of Senhora Graca. I was away from home this week, on a buying trip for my boss, the merchant Senhor Veloso, and only early last evening learned from Lazara what happened. I pushed my horse hard to arrive in time. I want to help you tame the saint."

Ponderously, Xexeo considered the application for a time, before delivering his immutable verdict.

"It is not possible. The blood of the white man flows in your veins. You would contaminate the matching saint we hope to raise, and possibly destroy our chance of success."

Caozinho slumped, and Chief Paiwe emerged from the audience to lay two conciliatory hands on the youth's shoulders.

"Your fate cannot be ours, son, but you can perform a role just as noble. Bear witness to this day, and then carry news of our sacrifice to the world."

This role seemed to cheer Caozinho, and he straightened his back and beamed.

Now began the final preparations for the hagiogeny of the village.

"We must bring the saint to the shore," Xexeo informed them. "Clear a path through the village."

Immediately, men, children and women began tearing down those robust but lightweight huts that intervened between the wagon and the track to the sea. Ixay approached the shaman.

"The wheels of the wagon will surely mire in the sand before we have advanced far."

"What do you suggest?"

"Dispose of the useless wheels and employ the bed of the wagon as a sledge."

"See to it!"

By mid-morning, all was in readiness: as if an unusually meticulous hurricane had passed, a traversable path of destruction now ran straight through the dwellings; and the wagon, unwheeled yet rehitched to the refreshed team of horses, lay like a sled on the ground.

A whip cracked, the team strained, and the saint began her final land journey in her current incarnation. The biggest villagers laid their shoulders against the stakes of the bed and added their efforts, while all the rest solemnly followed. Musicians played on drums and flutes a tune that mixed the emotions of the branches of the Dry

A MOUTHFUL OF TONGUES

Toad tree—love, despair and mourning—in their proper weights. Bullroarers, spun with frantic energy, overlay the tune with an apocalyptic burr.

Slowly, slowly, the procession covered the half-mile to the shore. Xexeo signalled a halt at the edge of the highest wave, instructing that the sledge be aligned so that its front pointed toward the water. This involved urging the reluctant horses into the breakers, and there was much revolt among the beasts before Tulikawa lent a cousinly hand. The team finally accomplished the task and were freed to gallop away.

A hundred huddled persons quietly awaited the shaman's next order. (Caozinho kept himself apart, where the beach grassed out.)

"Unveil the saint!"

Knots dissolved under nimble fingers, and the old sail was reefed away, from head to toe.

Charred countenance—plum birthmark overwhelmed—seared breasts, burnt belly, cooked thighs, scorched feet: judging by her injuries, all leaking or scabbed, the giant woman, big as some threescore men fused together, should surely have been dead, yet lay only in a coma disclosed by her slow breathing.

"Bring me the blade!"

An acolyte handed his master a sharp machete. Xexeo spoke to the listeners.

"We must be very precise. I will feed last those who have been chosen to launch the saint, so that they retain control of themselves long enough to send the saint on her way and rejoin us. Stand off to one side, you mighty crew, so that I may see you."

The brawniest villagers, including Ixay, segregated themselves.

"Very good. The rest of you may commence to file by me."

Xexeo moved to a flank of the giantess, laid a hand against her ruined meat like a butcher appraising a cut of beef, and then applied his knife.

The first communicant, an old woman with pendulous dugs, took the sliver of flesh hesitantly, but swallowed. When nothing happened immediately to her, the others followed suit more confidently.

Midway through the long communion, Tulikawa reached the head of the line. A shawled Yeena bestrode his back. Ixay cut two slices and handed them to the centaur, who passed one up to his rider. Smiling, they chewed the saint's flesh and moved on.

Before noon, all the villagers had consumed their portion of the saint, including the men appointed to push her into the sea. Only Xexeo had yet to partake.

The shaman threw down his staff and blade, and, with surprising agility, scrambled up onto the saint. Gaining purchase on her crisped stomach, he strode to her chin. Without hesitation he plunged both arms into her slightly parted lips and unmeeting teeth, as into a crevice. No reaction opposed him. Tugging manfully, he managed to pull the tip of her tongue into view. He leaned over and, with sharp teeth, bit off a mouthful of tongue and swallowed the chunk whole.

"Launch the saint!"

Heaving mightily, the crew slid the makeshift raft into the sea.

The first touch of brine sent a titanic shiver through the unconscious giantess, tumbling Xexeo off with a splash. Helped to his feet, sputtering, the shaman still insisted, "Float her deeply!" The men obeyed, pushing until their feet lost purchase on the sea bottom. When the saint was well afloat, the men paddled and lurched back to dry land.

Drifting further off, the saint began to heave about as if wracked by internal storms. Inevitably, a comber swamped the crude rocking raft, and it revolved like a log, sending the mangled woman below the surface and out of sight, ocean eddying around her disappearance.

Back on the shore, the villagers were moiling uneasily. Crusted with sand, Xexeo bellowed his ultimate command.

"Cluster round me! I am the seed!"

Obeying from custom and from new undeniable impulses, the villagers began to aggregate around their shaman, hiding him completely. Like sticky grains of rice, they clumped ever tighter around him, the outer ones fighting to penetrate deeper, like sperm targeting an egg.

From the marge Caozinho watched, transfixed by the magnitude of the transformation.

The riotous turmoil began to assume an extrahuman quality. Flesh lost its boundaries, neighbor melting into neighbor just as the whorish saint had sucked her patrons into herself. The carnal gravity of the protoplasmic ball eventually insured a terminal isotropy: like an immense stranded jellyfish, the entire tribe now resided in a featureless lump of living matter, its translucent integument blandly colored with adipose streaks, with shadowy organelles that were once humans half-seen floating inside.

Then the agglomeration, the proto-saint, began to change.

Paws protruded, claws unsheathed, cloaked penis lengthened, ears erected, whiskers wired, tail uncoiled, snout boxed out, spine snaked, eyes lamped green, black fur sprouted.

The gargantuan male jaguar, some hundred bodies large, pulled himself up into a sitting position. Calmly he regarded the ocean where the saint had sunk, tabby at a mousehole, the only sign of his emotions the slow sweep of his tail across yards of sand. (Caozinho too watched with trembling anticipation, standing on tiptoes.)

After some time, the spot of ocean under observation began to boil.

The tip of a krakenish tentacle broke the surface, sending the jaguar instantly to all fours. More of the long flexible limb emerged, tasting the air. Other sensitive tendrils began to agitate the sea. Folds of mantle and ruffled draperies of delicately tinted nautiloid flesh hove into view. Filamentary extrusions clasped and unclasped each other, multiple cilla whipped the innocent waves.

Revivified by its native element, the engineered benthic who shared an identity with Kerry Hackett churned powerfully, reveling in its health and freedom.

Like a housecat after a robin, the jaguar leapt then, landing many dozens of yards out from shore. He waded further, until waves soaked his glossy belly and he was within reach of the sea-creature that was his prey. With a decisive lunge, the jaguar captured a segment of the benthic in his jaws. The sea-creature, smaller than the predator, reacted wildly, wrapping itself around the jaguar's head.

Unable to see yet undaunted, the cat turned and struggled back toward the shore. When he could sense by the shallows that land was near, the jaguar simultaneously opened his jaws and whipped his head. The benthic soared through the air to crash in a patch of dense littoral vegetation.

Caozinho flinched at the passage of the benthic above his head, but did not run.

A minute passed without more than a crackling, humming noise from where the beached benthic had landed. Then, a stirring:

Ears gabled upward, eyes portholed, teeth picketed. A second feline head reared up from amidst the crushed trees, followed swiftly by the rest of the second black jaguar.

The two Olympian animals faced each other for an eternal second, snarling, low growls like the rumble of distant thunder their only exchange. Then the smaller jaguar that was Kerry Hackett turned and bolted, the estrus-red door of her animal cunt prominent.

The male jaguar whose constituents were the Dartpipe villagers launched itself after her.

Pawpads the size of couches, spray of saliva like a shower, reek like a musk factory: both animals brushed close enough by Caozinho to send him sprawling. By the time he found his feet, only the tips of their thrashing tails above the distant jungle were visible, accompanied by a crashing of trees.

Caozinho looked out to sea, at the empty beach, then back toward the deserted village, as if fixing his incredible memories even more indelibly. Then, with slow and thoughtful pace, he began his long journey home.

The trail of the mammoth jaguars through the jungle was wider than the road that led from the town, albeit less crisp. Smashed crowns and toppled boles, crushed animals, in a moist clearing pawprints big as a patio.

For some miles the smaller jaguar kept her lead, through thicket and copse, across streams and gullies. But the noise of her pursuer drew closer and closer. Laboring lungs pounded nearly against the molten anvil of her heart. Her eyes began to glaze with desperation.

Without foreknowledge, the lead jaguar crashed out of the jungle and halted at the edge of a broad savannah. Miles of grassy emptiness stretched away, offering no cover or impediment to pursuit.

She moved off a few dozen yards only, then turned to await the male.

A MOUTHFUL OF TONGUES

The Dartpipe jaguar burst out of the gap in the foliage and faced the female.

In an instant, both had reared up onto their hindpaws, towering over any tree. With a feral screech, the female hoisted a forepaw and cast a savage blow at the male. Claws raked his face, guttering blood, but he swiped awesomely in reply, his own claws mittened, clouting the female powerfully enough to upset her and send her sprawling. Then he was upon her. She rolled onto her back so as to rake and disembowel him, but he sprang to one side and fastened his mouth onto her soft corded neck, clamping but not puncturing, the female thwarted with only one forepaw nailed against her attacker's shoulder.

Thus they paused, unable to lock eyes, yet somehow, perhaps through medium of needling fang or gouging claw, communicating intentions and desires, testing willfullness against willfullness, matching strength to strength, flaw to flaw, complementarity to complementarity.

Movement signalled the end of this silent exchange.

The female retracted her claws.

Without releasing his captive completely, the male relaxed his own grip enough to let the female roll over onto her stomach while he simultaneously positioned himself above her. Her back arched in lordosis, his hindquarters couched themselves against hers.

Jaguar cock unslung itself and found its way to the gates of jaguar cunt.

When the gristly knot far down the pointy veined length crested the hot sloppy entrance, the male unmouthed his mate, just as she loosed a roar of triumphant defeat, pleasure mixed with despair, love with mourning.

Their first fuck lasted only a short rampageous time, tearing divots from the turf and sending nearby birds a-wing. But the initial dose of tutorial jism was almost immediately followed by a second and a third instruction.

Finally sated, they collapsed to the verdant grass, two lithe black jaguars lying entwined, licking each other's muzzles beneath the sun.

PART THREE

Large pale hands—blonde-haired and beringed, nails trimmed close—vee together to support a thick leather-skinned volume tailed with scarlet ribbons for place-marking. With a sharp clap, the hard-used book suddenly closes, revealing its palm-rubbed cover embossed with gold Gothic lettering.

The priest wears a blue plastic mack, shoulders pasted with small crumbling heaps of icy slush. His shoes crater the slop at graveside. His squarish ruddy face professionally hosts a vocational grief, as an athlete inhabits his uniform.

Sleet continues to sluice down from the scowling ashy heavens, a soft frigid pelting that heaps higher by degrees small tumuli of frozen water very close to phase-change, always just on the point of deliquescing, but never quite escaping the grip of winter.

The mourners around the priest, arrayed along the open mouth of the grave like some frieze of edifying monkeys, number only three:

Pock-faced Peter Jarius, elegant in thick Burberry tweed, holding a big incongruously striped golfing umbrella over himself and his receptionist, Oreesha Presser. Tearful in black, the African-American woman smudges her makeup further with a soppy tissue. Alongside these two, yet separate, stands Tango, his wasted yet still bulky frame slumped, his wet head uncovered and slightly bowed, hands thrust into pockets of a flame-painted motorcycle jacket.

An idling backhoe chugs softly some yards off, driver obscured behind steamy windows. Two overalled workers from the cemetery hang back from the grave until the priest nods them closer. They step forward and grip the revolving geared handles of the mechanism meant to lower the coffin into the earth.

The coffin sits suspended just above the clot-sided grave in its canvas sling, obscuring the tombstone already erected at the head of the plot.

"If we are finished with our prayers . . . " The priest's voice trails off. Since no one signals yay or nay, he flicks a finger at the laborers. They begin to crank.

As the coffin descends, the legend on the tombstone is revealed:

KERRY HACKETT
1990-2015

"Lost Angel of a ruined Paradise!
She knew not 'twas her own; as with no stain
She faded, like a cloud which had outwept its rain."
—Shelley

The coffin thunks bottom. The workers begin to wrestle up the slings in anticipation of their next use, and the driver of the backhoe races his engine chidingly.

"The service is now concluded," announces the priest. "Thank you all for honoring the memory of Ms. Hackett with your presence. If anyone wishes to speak further with me, I will be available in the chapel here for a short time, and then back in the city at my parish. Please drive safely. Conditions appear treacherous."

Umbrella bobbing responsively, Jarius follows his distraught employee as she heads swiftly but somewhat blindly for a limousine parked at the nearest juncture of cemetery roads. Tango does not accompany them, but cuts across the soggy lawn on foot, heading toward the main gate.

By the time the limo manages to turn around in the narrow lanes and advance down slippery macadam as far as the gate, Tango is already through the exit and heading down the cemetery drive. The car pulls up abreast of the walking man and the rear window powers down.

"Do you intend to walk all the way back to the city then, Mr. Santangelo?"

"There's a bus stop half a mile away. That's how I got here."

"It would be inhuman of me not to offer you a ride. And uncharitable of you not to accept."

"Are you teaching a fucking philosophy course, or asking me to get in the car?"

Jarius smiles wryly. "A glorious informality! What a fine start to the intimate conversation I would like us to have. By all mean, Mr. Santangelo, please hop inside."

Jarius levers his door open, and warmth puffs out into the greedy air. Tango slips inside.

Only Tango and Jarius occupy the broad rear seat. Up front, behind a soundproof glass panel, Oreesha Presser rides shotgun beside Anselmo, the driver. The woman continues circumspectly to weep in weird, glass-enforced silence, while the chauffeur shifts out of park and sends the limo down the long drive toward the main road.

At the intersection of drive and avenue, twin trees tower, memorial oaks. As the car takes the turn, behind one tree, as if undecided whether to hide or not, a shabby human figure lurks awkwardly, filthy face hooded in the folds of a synthetic blue blanket that also mantles the figure against the elements. The limo accelerates, leaving the odd interloper behind.

Jarius extends a hand to Tango, who responds with a perfunctory swipe.

"Despite sad circumstance having thrown us together, we have never previously been formally introduced, Mr. Santangelo. Yet I feel we know each other well."

"Maybe too well."

"Oh, such a condition could never obtain between two men who shared the love of a woman such as Ms. Hackett. And I realize I do flatter myself by such a tenuous nomination, although certain grounds for my enjoying such a privileged state do exist. In any case, I think we must get to know each other even better."

Red-eyed, unshaven, Tango simmers for thirty seconds, then blurts out, "You fucking killed her, you bastard! Admit it! Just between the two of us, right here, right now. You're the only reason Kerry's dead."

"Ah, Mr. Santangelo—admirably, you cut right to the heart of the discussion I wished to conduct. Let me begin by saying that no one is sadder than I at Ms. Hackett's untimely death. A bright and shining angel has been removed from this sorry mortal coil. But the onus for her sanguinary end lies almost exclusively at the feet of her own willful unpredictability. True, I erred to a small degree perhaps when I enrolled her as a privileged entrant to the high-security division of Diaverde. But granting such a clearance was well within my discretion. How could I possibly predict that *your* brutish behavior would drive her to utilize our invaluable experimental creation in an elaborate suicide?"

"What the hell are you saying? How did I drive Kerry to kill herself?"

"As you can well imagine, Mr. Santangelo, given the nature of Ms. Hackett's death, an extensive autopsy was conducted. Once the DNA of the Diaverde creation which she madly freed and spontaneously embraced—the 'benthic,' we termed it; alas, now expired along with Ms. Hackett, the only one of its kind lost forever—once this foreign material was separated out from Ms. Hackett's untidy corpse which night security found gracing the floor of the lab —well, we discovered some other non-self DNA in the remains of our unfortunate lady. Shall I put it bluntly, Mr. Santangelo, in the manner you favor? We pulled your sickly cum out of her ass."

Tango sits silently, discoloring the leather of the seat with the slush melting off him.

"Ah, you were not aware of this suggestive finding, were you? I thought not. I kept it quiet, you see. Diaverde had garnered enough awful publicity already without rumors of rape and assault being bruited about. And surely rape and assault must have been involved, Mr. Santangelo? I can't imagine that Ms. Hackett was in the habit of allowing a man with your level of viral infection unprotected anal intromission. Even if such contact weren't against the law—a law I'm certain you can quote by heart—I'm sure Ms. Hackett had more sense and regard for her own good health than that. It must have been very emotionally shattering to her when you took her in such a foul manner the very night of her self-destruction."

"Why are you bringing all this up now?"

"Only so that we both understand that a certain level of culpability adheres to each of us. I must live with the guilt of providing access to a tool of destruction, while you must live with the knowledge that your assault probably pushed your lover over the edge of sanity. Means and motive, we both share in Ms. Hackett's death."

A MOUTHFUL OF TONGUES

"So?"

"Just this: any legal or illegal actions you are contemplating against Diaverde or myself would surely boomerang against you, Mr. Santangelo. Neither one of us would emerge unscathed from public revelations of our roles. But this is not to say that we cannot reach a certain understanding. Ms. Hackett was a valuable employee, and as her significant other, it seems to me you deserve to collect a moderate yet fair amount of survivor's benefits—although no legal requirements for such a payment exist. Would seventy-five thousand sound about right to you?"

Tango chafes his right wrist with the fingertips of his left, as if his joints pained him. "Sure, why not. I don't have long to live anyhow, and that amount will grease the skids just fine."

Jarius rearranges his antique blemishes with a grin. "I took the liberty of cutting the check before the funeral. Here it is."

From pocket to pocket, the check flashes briefly. A certain tension almost visible during the discussion dissipates now. In the front seat, Oreesha Presser has ceased crying, and stares fixedly ahead. The driver navigates a semi-deserted freeway now, and the city looms in the distance, a brutalist poem in concrete and glass. Jarius and Tango sit almost companionably in silence, until Tango speaks.

"What was all that shit on her tombstone? Kerry never was into poetry that much."

"Ah, just my simple gesture, Mr. Santangelo. Since I personally paid for the stone, I felt it well within my perquisites to have an appropriate verse engraved upon it. Did you think it inapposite?"

"You're kidding yourself if you think Kerry was some kind of angel. She was just a person, as human as you or me."

"True enough, I suppose, despite my romantic illusions otherwise. But she retained even that humble status only up to the moment of her death. You saw her body at the morgue, Mr. Santangelo, after the benthic was finished with it. Would you call those shattered remains human?"

Tango shivers, and does not answer.

* * *

Pale light, pale faces: another dull and claustrophobic morning in the fraying city. Pedestrians, vendor carts and soldiers shuffle, wheel or stalk down the sidewalks, select vehicles of the elite share the mostly empty streets. A lackluster February sun lights the old dirty accumulations of ice and snow with a miser's charity. A lone pigeon struts along Brownian vectors, hunger supplying its quantum jolting.

On a mostly untraveled side street linking two main avenues (AMADOR STREET, its dangling sign proclaims), a chute of blank-faced ruins, the stoop of a plywood-windowed tenement hosts several rag-bundled winos passing a bottle of sweet port back and forth. In the midst of their drinking, an argument breaks out over an alleged unfairness: grimy hands snatch competitively at the bottle, purchase is lost, the bottle slips, smashes, and precious wine gushes out. Clumsily swatting each other, the winos arise and stalk off, presumably in search of more booze, or NUdollars convertible to same.

The abandoned shard-flecked pool of wine does not immediately freeze, nor does it shrink much through evaporation in the first minutes of its liberation. An intruder wind channeled down the street ruffles the lees, deposits a scrim of golden dust upon it, as pollen drops upon a lake, sheening it with fertile grains.

Moistened, the spores unpack their novel heritage. The spill deepens in color, ripples, quivers, and tosses a lariat of its new substance a few inches ahead, snaring a scrap of paper trash. Incorporating the trash, the pool assumes grander ambitions, and heaves its leading edge atop a curb-draped dead rat. The rat sublimates away, and the pool continues to enlarge itself.

By noon the side street hosts an irregular blot some hundred square feet in extent. The patch of mulberry-colored colloid is only a half-inch deep, and clings as easily to vertical surfaces—the risers of the steps, the tenement wall, the side of a busted hydrant—as it does to horizontal planes.

The first passerby to encounter the transubstantiated wine, a bicycle-riding messenger, considers it briefly before automatically swerving around it. The second and third people down the street, a man and a woman absorbed in talk, unwittingly traverse a shadowed portion of the patch, then stop and exclaim.

A MOUTHFUL OF TONGUES

"What's this sticky stuff?"

"Wine?"

"Someone must have spilled a whole case."

"Wish I had that kind of money."

They leave the scene behind, trailing some of the glop on their shoes.

The fourth person, an acned teenaged girl hoisting a garbage bag full of empty cans on her shoulder, encounters a qualitatively different scene.

The patch is practicing forms.

From its surface, like the fruiting bodies thrown upward by colonizing slime molds, the strange wine extrudes recognizable, though monotone shapes on the end of thallophytic stalks: an orchid flower, a melon, a pinnate leaf, a banana, a coconut. The shapes waver on the ends of their attachments for a few random moments, then are sucked back in to be replaced by new extrusions elsewhere across the surface. The overall effect is similar to an animated photomicrograph taken of a liquid under bombardment by pellets and casting up in response temporary castles and turrets out of its own body.

Cans clatter tinnily on pavement, escape confinement and roll off. Bagless, the scavenger girl runs.

Not long thereafter, soldiers arrive, perform a quick recon down the side street, then retreat, leaving an itchy-fingered guard at either end of the block.

Within half an hour, official barricades are in place, webcasters both independent and site-affiliated, kept frustratingly back at an official remove, are angling their digicams for their best possible shots, and a squad of technicians are donning bunnysuits, the transparent plastic panels of their hoods like computer monitors offering only unvarying extreme closeups of nervous faces.

* * *

A slowly trundling armored soundtruck, beetle without a dungball, circuits the chill and nighted city.

"Curfew is in effect until six AM. Violators will be shot on sight. Curfew is in effect—"

Minimally, the city's guardsmen roam paired. Some squads comprise a dozen members. All are equipped with a new style of grenade bandoliered in clusters.

One flak-jacketed Mutt and Jeff duo consists of two hard-faced women, an Hispanic and an Anglo, hiking with brave yet subtly unconvincing assurance down a block of steel-shuttered shops. Boots tromp the urban silence into its grave, but the pair remain unspeaking until the petite Hispanic nudges a silver egg topped with a failsafe triggering mechanism that dangles from her chest.

"You think these things will take out the creeping crud?"

"Doubt it. The mayor still hasn't declared Amador Street sterilized yet, has he?"

"Why the fuck are we even carrying them then?"

"They're military rabbit's-feet. You rub them and all your jagged nerves go away."

"I wish to hell they did even that much."

Spectral movement across a near-lightless block: the carbon-paper cutout of a lone soldier creeping from coign to coign.

"Halt!"

The single figure straightens and breaks into a lope. The women raise their rifles, snapping off several rounds. No debilitating shot intercepts the loner, who escapes down an uninviting alley.

"That was the Rogue Soldier!"

"You think so? Old whatsisname?"

"Shangold."

"Is he any more than a legend? How could he have survived all this time on his own? The whole city is against him."

"He's a mean and shifty bastard. Rapes women and steals their money, lives on the street and stays on a permanent honey-high."

"Should we go after him?"

"Fuck no! I've got two kids, and they don't pay us enough for the kind of nasty shit that makes orphans!"

Down the handy alley that warrens other musty trash-packed channels the fugitive races, leaving the patrols behind. Stray gleams of wasted luminance from security lamps, streetlights and penthouse apartment windows jigsaw big shoulders, hectic eyes, black cheeks, a trouser's broken zipper pinned shut. The Rogue Soldier stops by a certain dumpster collaged with graffiti tags, slides open a side door, and thrusts his arm in. He rummages for a while before pulling out a cached package. Opened, the plastic bundle disgorges a waxy honeycomb, its cells capped with artificial red gelatin. Private Shangold bites hungrily into the mass, and viscous gold syrups his chin. He crams everything down, swiping his chin with tongue and finger, licking the inner surface of the dumpster-stashed paper for any minute traces of his fix.

"Private Shangold, how I've missed you."

Bright eyes wide in his black face, Shangold whirls, firing a long burst through a half-circle of empty space.

"No, Private—right here behind you."

Ten leaky needles, two paired sets of green fingernails, pierce Shangold's neck. He stiffens, drops his gun, and folds to the soiled pavement, eyes still open beneath brim of helmet.

Breath puffing visibly, yet seemingly untroubled by the cold, Kerry Hackett, naked as raw ore torn from the earth, steps into Shangold's limited field of vision, a foreshortened surreal montage of thighs, cunt, belly, breasts and face.

"Do you remember this particular me, Private? A lot of me's went away for a while, in a lot of worlds, and a lot of me's stayed behind, in a lot of other worlds. The ones that stayed didn't do too good. But the ones that went away did wonderful. Does your memory extend across all the different worlds? Mine does. But maybe my mouth will help you remember all the me's."

Kerry steps over the recumbent paralyzed soldier and squats. Irresistible hands pop the safety pin and waist-snap off his pants and tear the fabric down to his knees. His shorts are soon similarly shredded, and his tremulous cock lolls into view.

Kerry glissades a wet fingertip down the length of his dick, and the hefty cock seems almost to suction blood into itself, a black swan's neck unfurling out of sleep. Kerry palms the prick, lowers her face and applies only the teeth-framed tip of her tongue to its hole. Her tongue adheres to the cock head, detaches, and begins to force an entry into the fleshy tube. Compressed yet still nearly as wide as Shangold's dick itself, the autonomous tongue burrows into the urethral slot. Soon the root of the tongue disappears within the distorted cock head, as the concealed forepart continues to tunnel inward. The passage of the tongue through the penis is visible as a sliding, humping bubble, evocative of a pig's passage down a python.

Kerry rips off Shangold's jacket and shirt, exposing his torso as if he were a dinner out of a microwave, then steps back.

After a few minutes, Shangold's skin begins to acquire a taut reptilian patterning, an epidermal tessellation, as if the Rogue Soldier stood revealed as some sort of were-gator. But his transformation, it is soon evident, is not into a single other being, but into many.

Living lizard heads, all flaring nostrils and gozzling eyes, form first as bas-reliefs across Shangold's waffled verdigris midriff, pectorals and thighs. The heads push up, dragging bodies with them, elastically exiting Shangold's body as if it were a membrane-topped pool, assuming a rugged and happy three-dimensionality as their last claw separates.

Eschering out of Shangold, the whip-tailed lizards inevitably take much of the man's mass with them, and his body deflates to something like a punctured inner tube. As the first generation separate completely from the man, he lies reduced by a third.

Miraculously, apparently through some calculated preservation of his inner vital organs, as wasps maintain their egg-hosts, Shangold remains alive, a state betokened by quivering breaths and alert eyes.

But a second round of births (the original lizards are already dispersing into the city streets, tongues tasting freedom) inevitably claims his life, leaving only an amorphous functionless nubbin attached to the adult head.

The third spawning—only three small lizards in this final litter —spares only the dead head and a cord of twitching gristle partially mimicking a spine.

Kerry laughs and kicks the mortal remnant into the air. Helmet drums against dumpster, then bonks to ground. She strides off on bare feet, popping a small glass bottle beneath her sole without concern.

* * *

The groundfloor entryway to Kerry's old apartment building—doorlock perpetually unfunctioning, tight space lit by a low-wattage yellow bulb—shelters a blanketed lump, blue synthetic felt tinged to green. Snores filter past the fabric, and damped-down oneiric actions tug at the unseen sleeper's muscles, jittering the blanket's lines and revealing the duct-taped toe of an old boot.

Delicately formed yet impervious bare feet transit scarred gritty linoleum, pause beside the sleeper. A green-nailed hand descends and tugs the blanket down.

In a bearded, sunken-cheeked face layered with grime to an indeterminate shade and texture, street-seasoned eyes flutter open. A smile swiftly accompanies the awakening.

"You gave me some money once. But I heard you were dead."

"You helped me once. And I'm not dead."

"How come you got no clothes on? Am I dreaming? This sure feels like a dream."

Kerry drops down beside the beggar. "Don't ask me questions. I don't answer questions. Let me listen at your chest."

"You some kind of doctor or social worker? Oh, sorry, I forgot. Sure, why not?"

Five layers of greasy clothing at first resist clumsy unfastening by frost-warped hands, but yield to Kerry's dissolving touch.

"Hey, I need all my shirts to keep warm! And you got me all wet somehow! What'd you spill on me?"

"Don't worry. I'll bring you some new dry clothes on my way out. Now lie back."

The beggar's blistered chest is a Golgotha of pus-rimmed fumaroles, a plain of decay. A foul atmosphere wafts upward off this blasted land.

Kerry places her birthmark flat against the devastation, listens attentively, then raises her face.

"Kiss me."

"Lady, I don't want any trouble with your man—"

"Shut up."

Soft hairless lips mash chapped and fringed ones, and a peristaltic wave tsunamis down the beggar's throat, jogging his sharp Adam's apple. Mouths break apart, and the man says, "Hey, you slipped me something!"

"It's going to fix you up inside. Let me soothe your skin too."

Kerry begins luxuriantly to massage the wasted chest, and the beggar relaxes backwards, eyes closed. She works downward, spreading a translucent autocatalyzed film across his wounds. When she reaches his waist, multiple pairs of pants are easily slipped over bony hips.

Kerry applies gel out of her palms across the beggar's thin flanks, then grips his limp prick.

"I can't get it up no more these days, lady—"

"Shut up."

Within seconds, the beggar's astonished grunts greet the revival of his erection.

Kerry positions herself over the man, vaginally sockets home his prick up to his scrannel balls, and commences a motionless extraction of his seminal essences.

As soon as she has the beggar's cum, Kerry's up and onto her feet.

"Wait here for me."

"Lady, I couldn't go anywhere now if I wanted to. I feel too funny, and I got no clothes . . . "

A webcast pushes itself out of the hair-thin glass pipes inside Tango's dim apartment and through a monitor, depicting a floodlighted street scene: plastic barricades behind which tower swaying tropical trees in vibrant jade, lime, olive and chartreuse.

"—further contaminated areas. Having resisted all attempts to exterminate them, the oldest areas of contamination are now exhibiting a new behavior described by experts as 'ecopoiesis.' Full vegetative environments are arising where only undifferentiated purple pools of change-agent were once observed—"

Tango emerges naked from the bathroom, toweling his wet hair. His physique shows the traces of past strength and grace ravaged by his illness. He stands before the monitor to watch the newscast.

Two arms wrap around his midsection from behind, and Kerry presses herself against him, her bush to his ass, her breasts to his back.

"Did you miss me, dear?"

Momentarily medusa'd, Tango's face cracks at last into fearful fragments.

"You—you're dead."

"Why does everyone believe that? Would a dead woman have a warm hard prick like mine?"

Tango's breathing stutters, and his hips jerk. He tries to break free, but is gripped all the tighter: ribs creak, and he winces.

A MOUTHFUL OF TONGUES

"I don't know how you're alive or why you're here, but I'm asking you not to put whatever you've got there in me."

"Why not? Isn't that what you like? Look, you're getting hard yourself." One arm still banding her quarry, Kerry reaches around to grab Tango's virally malformed cock and pump it. "Your ass want me. Look, I'll prove it."

Kerry's bumps her pelvis forward, plunging her cock up Tango's asshole, and her old roommate yelps.

"Don't be a baby, my dick was wet enough. Now, just relax, dear."

"Kerry, if you love me—"

"Oh, I love you, Tango. Just not the way you are."

Without hip-thrusts, Kerry nonetheless quickly discharges herself up Tango: a droplet or two of plentiful ejaculate escapes Tango's ass to spatter on the floor.

"I want to hold you while my cum works. Here, I'll bring you off too while we wait. One last time, to show there's no hard feelings."

Pinned and frightened, Tango cannot resist. Kerry works the man's noduled cock until he sprays across the monitor. Cum drips down the screen, prisming the colors beneath, melting the face of the newscaster like a candle.

The trapped man's skin abruptly parchments. Wings begin to emerge from his transfigured integument, small papery insect wings that assume the painted markings of a dozen different species-specific constellations as they blossom.

Tango is decomposing into butterflies, just as the Rogue Soldier mumped out in lizards.

The shy insects are reluctant to fly far at first. They remain perched or gently hovering close to their place of birth, like monarchs clustering in a eucalyptus forest. Butterfly by butterfly, Tango is soon shrouded completely from view. Kerry maintains her embrace, but it now appears that she is clutching only a quivering chromatic, human-shaped heap of butterflies, their wings oscillating in chaotic patterns.

After a time, Kerry steps back without unlinking her arms, pulling them through the lepidopterous space that Tango once occupied. The man-shaped mass of butterflies trembles, but does not yet fall apart. Kerry steps to a window and hefts the lower sash upward. Chill air blasts in, and the column of butterflies shatters. No man is left behind. Flittering en masse, they pour out the window into the night.

Kerry disappears into her old bedroom. She returns with an armful of Tango's clothing, her charitable donation for the day, and lets herself out.

* * *

Gowned and slippered, sipping a brandy, Peter Jarius sits on a leather couch in his apartment, reading beneath the light of a Tiffany floorlamp, its Arcadian shade a window onto some bright elysian pasture. Quiet symphonic music plays, but not loudly enough to cover the sound of something breaking upon the floor, a toppled vase or glass perhaps. Jarius drops his book and rockets to his feet.

"Who's there? I can have security here instantly!"

Movement in a dark corner: two amber feline eyes rather high off the floor cast back the candied light before disappearing.

Nervous laughter seeks release. "Only a cat. Some neighbor's cat!"

Jarius discovers he's still holding his tumbler, swigs a mouthful of bronze, then drops back down upon the sofa, landing in Kerry's lap.

"My Christ!" Splashed with brandy, the man picks himself partially up off the carpet (an older stain marks a previous spill), managing to assume an all-fours position before the sight of Kerry's prominent cunt halts him.

Spraddle-legged on the sofa, Kerry smiles. She leans forward, breasts gamboling, and holds forth something in her hand.

Drape of white leather, welt of silver zipper, irregular cutout.

"I'll wear your mask now, Peter. The thought of it doesn't frighten me at all."

Jarius seems pinned in place, and finding his tongue takes moments. Nonetheless, he summons up a meager share of his wonted assurance. "Reports of your death were greatly exaggerated, I see. I hope you approved of your tombstone. It was the best money could buy. Can I assume the benthic—"

"You can assume whatever you want. But the important question is, do you still want me?"

A MOUTHFUL OF TONGUES

"Why, of course, of course, my dear. Certainly I want you. Perhaps even more than before. A woman who has passed through death and beyond—there's a positive radiance about you, an actual aura. But I question whether this is the time and the place. Are the circumstances exactly conducive to—?"

"You've chosen. I'll put the hood on now."

Creamy calfskin mask, two small nostril holes its only concession to human frailty, replaces feminine features; the ratcheting whisper of a smooth zipper sounds as Kerry reaches behind her head.

Through its intended window, her birthmark blazes, a spill of Tyrian dye against a snowbank, lone exposed eye seeming to belong to a buried avalanche victim bleeding upward into arctic coverlet.

Jarius is transfixed. Kerry rises off the couch and closes the small gap between them. She reaches down and plucks Jarius by his hair, drags his face up into her lowered cunt.

Licking tentatively at first, then more excitedly, Jarius presses his mouth against Kerry's inner labia. But when he tries to shift position for better access, to pull his head back, he finds that he is stuck as on flypaper, mucilaged tight.

Now Kerry's orchidaceous cunt lips begin wetly to spread and sprawl, growing to cover Jarius's nose and chin, to film his cheeks. Desperately, the man places both hands against Kerry's thighs, dimpling her flesh, and pushes. With a ripping sound he separates from his hooded executioner. But the creeping caul of cunt flesh still crawls his skin. He reaches up in an attempt to claw it off, but the leading edges of the living mask offer no purchase, bonded tight to his own flesh. When the seething film bridges his eyes, Jarius topples over backward to the carpet, writhing.

The leather mask Kerry wears melts into her underlying face, and the zipper, still intertoothed, falls to the rug. The woman puts a hand between her legs and teases newly extruded labia into a comfortable, workable position.

Jarius's struggles have ceased. Below the consuming caul, his head is losing definition and substance. And beneath his robe, other struggles are underway: a rounded object pushes and bumps, seeking to escape the confines of expensive cloth. There is a jab, and the tip of some-thing sharp emerges. Slashing, a big razored beak breaks into the air, quickly followed by the head of a large par-rot, all blues, yellows and reds, a feathered rainbow. Le-vering itself out the rent fabric with its wings, the parrot is soon completely free. It half-flaps, half-hops across the floor to the tipped glass, samples droplets of Jarius's brandy, shakes its head, then begins to preen.

Bird by bird, Jarius becomes other than what he once was, leaving humanity behind for multiple incarnations into simpler souls.

Seven parrots make a man.

Kerry invites the wintry city air to host her tropical flock. The parrots wing quickly away, heading for the oasis of ecopoiesis visible not far off.

* * *

Multiple winey birthmarks on a concrete face, pools of purple change-agent in various stages of development speckle the city. Seen from above, the noncontiguous oases are plainly yearning toward their neighbors, ulti-mately intent on fusing into a single jungle.

In pre-dawn exclusivity, through a district of cheap yet well-maintained apartments, a naked woman strides down the sidewalk. At a certain building, she enters and climbs stairs to a third-floor apartment. There, she po-litely knocks.

The door opens several inches on its chain, and a slice of womanly black face becomes visible—one eye, half a nose and mouth—followed by the face's abrupt disap-pearance and a loud thump.

Kerry grips the arc of brass chain and tugs: links pop. She pushes the door against the unconscious body, slid-ing the fallen woman across the floorboards just enough to allow entrance.

Inside, Kerry picks up Oreesha Presser and carries her to a sofa-turned-bed. She lays the African-American woman down on the thin mattress. Oreesha wears only a flannel robe, and it's come disarrayed. Kerry peels back its halves to disclose Oreesha's body: conical tits with smudged graphite areolae and the dark Alexandrian delta of her loins. Kerry leans forward and swabs the in-side of the black woman's mouth with her tongue.

A MOUTHFUL OF TONGUES

Oreesha awakens, and scrabbles up to a sitting position against the pillows.

"You've really missed me."

Wide-eyed, Oreesha says, "Girl, if you aren't a ghost, then you've got a hell of a lot of explaining to do."

"I can't tell you what's happened to me, I have to show you. I've been somewhere special, and I want you to join me there."

"Someplace better than this hard, crazy life?"

"Yes. A beautiful green world."

"And what do I have to do to get to your Oz? Sell my soul?"

"No. Just lick my cunt."

Oreesha snorts. "I've heard that one before."

"Oh, but it won't be like you imagine. Watch."

Kerry's hands and knees meet the hard scratched floorboards. Her inviting cunt bisects Oreesha's view of her rear. Oreesha reacts by leaning forward, plainly intrigued at the temptation of Kerry's sex despite her initial dismissive reaction.

"Not yet," Kerry commands.

Her form has begun to waver.

Feet and hands don clawed paws, a playful tail hawsers out from her coccyx, thighs and forearms rearrange their musculature, black fur cloaks human skin.

But the transformation stops just below Kerry's breasts. Human above that line, jaguar below, she now crouches sphinx-like in hybrid glory.

Kerry turns her head back to gauge Oreesha's reaction. The woman has not averted her gaze, but instead remains riveted to her magicked friend.

"Now. Now you can lick me."

Wordlessly, Oreesha joins Kerry on the floor, black breasts dipping. Kerry lofts her hindquarters. Oreesha closes her eyes and drives her face forward, mashing her rich lips against the aromatic feline cunt, as if to conquer doubt and fear forever by one impulsive surge and strike.

"Oh, yes, that's so nice. Somebody started me earlier, but he never finished. Use your tongue."

Oreesha pulls back to extend her tongue, but already it's not her own.

It's a jaguar's broad facile strop.

Continuing to lick, the black woman loses her familiar shape also, wave by wave, exchanging it for a form that

179

sisters Kerry's. A final gestalt of change ripples over both women, extending upward from their animal-human interface, leaving them complete jaguar twins.

The rear jaguar continues to lap at the lead one's cunt, rousing purrs, growls, and a final howl.

At that moment the gapped door swings wider, and a third, bigger jaguar appears. The two females abandon sexual pleasuring for the moment and lope toward him; he turns, and all three trot down the stairs.

The front door of the apartment building, already swamped with brick-clinging lianas, gives onto a thicket of riotous vegetation lit by a turbulent rising sun. Lizards dart, butterflies flitter and parrots chatter at dawn's arrival. Beneath the slapping paws of the three jaguars, cement segues to packed earth, and they saunter boldly off.

Into that deep, dark, dangerous dream.

Providence,
February-July, 1999.